The Unbearable Sadness of Zilch

A Novella

Book Two of the Post-Lux Trilogy

Konrad Ventana

iUniverse, Inc.
New York   Bloomington

The Unbearable Sadness of Zilch
A Novella

iUniverse books may be ordered through booksellers or by contacting:

iUniverse
1663 Liberty Drive
Bloomington, IN 47403
www.iuniverse.com
1-800-Authors (1-800-288-4677)

Because of the dynamic nature of the Internet, any Web addresses or links contained in this book
may have changed since publication and may no longer be valid. The views expressed in this work
are solely those of the author and do not necessarily reflect the views of the publisher, and the
publisher hereby disclaims any responsibility for them.

ISBN: 978-1-4401-5824-7 (sc)
ISBN: 978-1-4401-5826-1 (hc)
ISBN: 978-1-4401-5825-4 (ebook)

Printed in the United States of America

Library of Congress Control Number: 2009932273

iUniverse rev. date: 10/12/2009

Acknowledgments

The author acknowledges the artistic contribution of Lewinhall Studios who provided the photographic frontispieces expressly for this novella. The cover art was derived from an original photograph provided by iStockphoto. The book's story and characters are fictitious, and the cinematography is imaginary.

Contents

Book Two

The Unbearable Sadness of Zilch

1. With Fingers to Their Lips

No one is innocent ... not in this town. In this town, the apocalypse has come and gone, lifting the veil of innocence like a great velvet curtain in an old movie house, where the only victims that don't return for the sequel are the gods themselves, struck out long ago by the big blue pencil. In this town, every man, woman, and child takes the limits of his or her own field of vision to be the limits of the world. Without the lamplights of fate that flicker in a constant state of anxiety through yonder movie reels, the collective vision would be blacker than the slate of a director's clapboard, suffused with a pessimism that goes far beyond film noir, far beyond existential anguish, far beyond the pale of postmodernism to the very crux of the loneliness, dread, and despair that is the wretched birthright of the descendent species.

No one is beatific ... not in this town. In this town, the *Panorama du Film Noir Américain* has come home to roost, elevating the morally ambivalent, the psychologically strange, the post-Freudian oneiric, the fatalistically cruel, and the contemptuously erotic to new cinematic heights before plunging expressionistically to its reiterative death in a declining series of swan dives off the towering hieroglyphs of HOLLYWOODLAND. In this sepulchre by the sea, the boundaries that divide real life from mere living death are, at best, shadowy and vague. That immortal instinct within the spirit of mankind that senses the *Beautiful* as it aspires to the divine is viewed nowadays as the desire of the moth for the star. There is no longer any such appreciation of the eternal, no wild effort to reach the elusive *Beauty above*, but a cool satisfaction with the garish *Beauty before us*, arrayed in disproportions approaching vice, with a snarling animosity for sentiments of supernal loveliness whose very elements appertain to eternity alone.

Some might call me cynical, due to a prevailing misinterpretation of the term. And while I do test very high on social criticism, I do not carry a lantern in the daytime; nor am I looking for an honest man—just a paying client with the weight of the world on his shoulders, someone I can help along the way in the same manner that Aristotle helped Alexander before he was *Great*, helped him with applied philosophy and practical counseling to better understand and/or alleviate the anxieties and emotional troubles that might otherwise have prevented him from achieving his true measure of *Greatness*. From the lonely captain of industry to the aging starlet to the gambler plum out of luck, Philosophical Counselors like me are the time-honored physicians of a given culture—we offer applied philosophy as medicine to ease the sickness and the suffering of the humans in the race. And in case you think my job is some kind of modernistic, New Age mumbo jumbo, consider for a moment that the medieval bestseller, *The Consolation of Philosophy* by Boethius, was originally written as a practical manual for inmates who, forsaken by fortune, were condemned to life, as it were, on death row.

"Dr. Joseph Metropolis, PhD, LPC, Philosophical Counselor," that's what the man said—just like it reads in big gold letters on the window of the door of my seedy office on Los Feliz Boulevard in Hollywood. That's what the man said just before he barged into my office and slammed the door behind him.

"You must be Joe Metropolis. I'm Zero Vaynilovich, and I need to speak with you immediately, if not sooner." Without offering his hand or waiting for an invitation, the impatient man pulled a nearby armchair even closer to my desk and seated himself accordingly, if not politely.

"Please, have a seat Mister Vaynilovich. What can I do for you today?"

"You can call me Zilch for starters, and don't get smart with me; I eat guys like you for breakfast. I'm here because I want you to do something for me ... something personal." He spoke with the authority of someone who was used to getting his own way.

"Go on," I said, sizing up the fit of the audacity with the physique of the middle-aged man. His aggressiveness was obviously tailored by

2

hand, and the fit was perfect. But something told me this sharp-dressed Hollywood executive was wearing a pair of cement overshoes.

"I'm a very important man in this town, a real big shot, if I do say so myself." Zilch glanced around the office as if to compare his lofty appointment with the meagerness of its trappings. My walls contain but one photo, and I choose to decorate with nothing more than a solid oak bookcase to hold my most-often-accessed books. "I have several thousand people who work for me," Zilch continued, "and when I tell them to do this or that, they do it, and quick!"

"I see," I said as I focused on that dull glimmer of helplessness that stood defiantly in the furrows between the blackness of his pupils and the dull metallic gray of his muscular irises that locked on to you like a Saturday-night special in a dark alley.

When a prospective client is talking to you, you listen to what he says with his eyes. It might seem strange to say, but the luminous world is a nearly invisible world; the luminous world is that which we do not often see. In the words of a French playwright, "*Our eyes of flesh see only noir.*" The demands of luminosity, like the demands of truth, are severe. She has no sympathy for either pretense or myrtles. All that is indispensible in public relations is all that she has nothing to do with. To deck her in flowery robes is to render her a harlot. It is but making her a flaunting paradox to bridle her with rhinestones and satin and lace and fine silk stockings. In the process of seeking this elusive luminosity, we verify our gifts of insight and intuition. In probing for these psychological truths, we descend from metaphorical supposition; we become simple and distinct. In the words of Edgar Allan Poe, patron saint of the detective-fiction genre, "*To convey 'the true' we are required to dismiss from the attention all inessentials.*"[1] To find true luminosity, we must become, in a word—Perspicuous!

"I need for you to find something for me—a beautiful woman actually—and I need you to understand that this is a very private matter."

"Perhaps what you need is to hire a Private Detective to find this woman," I said.

---

1   Poe's review of Longfellow's *Ballads and Other Poems,* from *Graham's Magazine.*

"I could hire a hundred Private Detectives to find anything I want. In Hollywood, we do it all the time. We hire detectives to dig up dirt on our enemies and our more troublesome business associates—then we leak the news of these clandestine operations along with the provocative inferences of slander and innuendo to one or two sleazy news reporters who then become the center of media attention, which only serves to focus everyone's attention on the dirty laundry and the immersion journalism that ultimately spirals out of control, eventually taking its toll on our adversaries and putting someone like me in a more favorable position of negotiation."

"I know. I read the newspapers," I said, trying not to yawn as I watched the flakes of ash from a previous client's cigarette float up out of the brass ashtray and crawl deliberately across the shiny top of my desk in the draft from an open window.

"Then you know that I could hire a hundred Private Detectives to find her—and maybe I will." Zilch swept the diverting ash trail off the desk and onto the floor with one swift movement of his empty hand. "Meanwhile, I want you to do something for me that I can't do for myself, something that only the likes of you and your ilk can do."

"Why me? There are lots of well-qualified therapists, shrinks, and life coaches in Hollywood. There are those who specialize in grief counseling, illness and loss, even anger management, which in your case might be recommended. You strike me as a man who knows what he wants and has pretty much figured out how to get what he wants." I met his gray gaze as I continued. "You're not a man who needs a reminder of the simplistic screenplay, *She's Just Not That Into You,* and I don't intend to hold your hand during your reality check."

"Don't give me that shit! I was the sun and the stars to her. She was completely in love with me, and I was totally into her." As Zero Vaynilovich spoke, his metallic eyes appeared to moisten and his brusque demeanor softened appreciably. "I know it sounds corny, but we were made for each other, and she would be the first to tell you so! Something happened that I can't explain; something just snapped. I know that we had some difficulties, we're both high-strung and demanding, but we always reconciled, eventually, that is."

"That is, until now."

"Yeah, until now. And I just can't stand it!"

"But why me, Mister Zilch? There must be some reason you sought me out."

"God damn it! You wrote *The Book*, and you know it." Zilch slammed his hands down hard on the desk, and then he stood up abruptly and walked to the open window, breathing deeply and shaking his head from side to side. When he turned back to face me, accusation flared in his eyes. "You know exactly why I'm here, and it sure isn't your bedside manner—it's that goddamned book of yours!"

Ahhhh, *The Book*, my **Lost Angels Pantheon**; I might have known. *The Book* that Zilch refers to with such enthusiasm was the culmination of my entire doctoral dissertation, six years of internship at the Malibu Drug Rehabilitation and Addiction Treatment Center, three years of teaching at the University of Philosophical Research, and another four years of intensive counseling with the Hollywood Suicide and Crisis Hotlines.

Before I wrote **Lost Angels Pantheon**, I was just another know-it-all with some additional letters after my name, but after *The Book*, things were different. People began to recognize themselves in the psychological archetypes and mythological motifs that I systematically categorized. It was as if, by describing the psychic pantheon of a litany of lost souls, I was describing the personal philosophical crises of a host of representative celebrities of our postmodern world of entertainment: their erosion of values, their spiritual disorientation, and what we in the business call metaphysical vertigo, which results in intense suffering from an interminable feeling of emptiness, along with a compelling desire to search for more reliable guiding principles. To put it mildly, I was mobbed after I wrote the book of the lost angels, mobbed to the point that I am inclined to travel around this town incognito.

"Now, now, Mister Zilch, perhaps it would be best if you did hire a competent Private Detective who could find this particular woman for you, and then he or she could initiate a dialogue between the two of you."

"That's not going to happen. I want you, the great Joe Metropolis, to help me." The dull gray Saturday-night specials attempted to hone in on their target as I parried the thrust.

"But come now, Mister Zilch," I said dismissively. "You know that love fades, reality sets in, people change right before our eyes. I can recommend some excellent clinical psychologists who specialize in marital relations, the agonies of heartbreak, and the associated problems of self-esteem."

Finally, the Saturday-night specials came alive; they drew a steady bead on me, and then they fired.

"Look here, Metropolis, you're not listening to what I'm telling you. For someone who's paid to listen, you're no damn good at it! I don't want to know WHERE she's run off to. What I really want … what I really *need* to know is WHY!!!"

"I see," I said, closely examining the sheer intensity of his gaze, and this time I really meant it. "Go on, don't stop now."

"I hate to admit it, but you're my last hope. Suddenly, I feel all dead inside."

"Go on."

"I feel like I'm backed up into a dark corner and I don't even know who or what's hitting me."

"I can sympathize with your dilemma, Mister Zilch, but before I can commit my services to this case, I want to be certain that you realize standard psychological counseling is always available to you. I need to be assured that you are fully aware of this, for professional reasons."

"No, I won't do it," he said, barely warding off defeat as he slumped back into the chair. "I won't submit to it, I tell you. I'm telling you now, once and for all, and in the strictest confidence, that I don't want any ordinary counseling. I want to know WHY! *Why* I feel like I'm dying all the time. *Why* she left me in the first place. *Why* she's not coming back. I want to know *why* my love was not strong enough to keep her." He paused momentarily, as if he was struggling somewhere between defiance and submission. Then out it came: "And besides breaking my heart, she stole something very valuable from me, and I want it back!"

I simply nodded in affirmation, for I had heard enough and seen enough to engender a necessary degree of sympathy for the man named Zilch. So I'm his last best hope. He's lost his gal, and he feels all dead inside. He's backed up into a dark corner, and he doesn't know who's hitting him. It's like I've heard this all before, like the voice of a hard-boiled Private Detective in an old black-and-white movie reel. Only now, in the ultra-neo-noir of our contemporary high society, it is not the *Private Eye* who is called upon to find some hidden Truth, it is the *Perspicuous Eye* who is called upon to find the lost Beauty.

It is somehow fitting for the important and impatient man named Zilch to eschew both the linear fact-finding mission of the stalwart Private Detective and the verbal arabesques of the tedious talking cures in favor of the dynamic maneuvers of the Philosophical Counselor who, like a knight on a chessboard, can move at once in both a linear and a tangential fashion, jumping over any hurdles that may lie in its path while surmounting substantive obstacles that would be impossible for any other chess piece on the board. The only real problem with this theory is that Philosophy is not a game for knights.

"What, may I ask, is this valuable thing that has presumably been stolen from you?"

"No, you may not ask. It's much too personal to discuss at this time. It's enough that I tell you something very valuable has been stolen from me, and I want it back."

"I heard you the first time, Mister Zilch. I'm simply trying to clarify the assumptions and parameters related to issues of meaning, value, and purpose."

"Cut the crap, Metropolis! You'll have plenty of opportunity to philosophize on your own time. On my time, I want you to work *for* me, not *on* me. I want you to drop everything you're doing, and I want you to start right away. I'll pay you double your going rate and all reasonable expenses. I want you to come to my house in Beverly Hills tonight, and I want you to come alone. It's on Crescent Drive," he said as he handed me his personal card with an address and a phone number and nothing else.

I managed at least one perfunctory nod and a customary offering of my professional business card before he began talking again.

"Come to my house at nine o'clock. I'll tell you everything you need to know."

As Zero Vaynilovich rose from the chair with my business card in his hand and proceeded to depart from the premises, he turned to me with a sheepish grin and inquired with uncharacteristic politeness, "By the way, what are you going to call this case? I know guys like you always come up with a clever title."

"I think I'll call this one ***The Lost Love of the Latest Tycoon.*** What do you think?"

"I think it will do just fine."

2. The Reddish Blue Dahlia

In a city where everyone drives everywhere, it often pays to walk a block or two, or even a mile, in whatever shoes one happens to find oneself in. I was thinking of this Zilch character as I was walking past the beige and white-washed apartment buildings of Los Feliz Boulevard, beneath the vicariously blinking eyes of the Griffith Observatory, down the declivitous sidewalks of Hillhurst Avenue. I thought of him as I passed the local hangouts, the boutiques and bourgeois bohemian cafes, on my way to the Alcove, where you could sit on the patio undisturbed, eating a turkey burger or a brie and apple panini or an Asian scallop salad, and think while the exhausted sun seems to hesitate for a moment in *illud tempus*[2] before stepping off the ledge of the horizon, leaving the world that much darker in the meantime. I was trying to remember who it was who had once said that *"the darkness of death is like evening twilight,"*[3] because it makes all objects appear more lovely … more lovely to the dying, that is. Failing that, I was trying to imagine exactly what kind of *misappropriated object* could possibly have aroused so much angst in a man like Zero Vaynilovich; a man who appears, at least on the surface, to already possess everything that a man could possibly want, and whatever he didn't already have, he could either rent or buy or place under contract.

As the giant purple bruise of the evening sky turned to more sinister shades of gray, the marine layer began to roll in with its attendant chill, reminding me that I was also under contract, so to speak, and that I had an anxious client waiting for me at the lovelier end of Sunset Boulevard. I gulped down the last remnants of my noodle salad and

---

2   Sacred time, now and always.
3   Quote from Jean Paul Richter.

the dregs of my double espresso and started back up the hill, where my wheels-of-the-week was parked underground.

I checked the time—it was eight forty-five—when I pressed the etched glass starter button on the shadow-gray coupe. The crystal lit bright red, and the V-12 roared to life, then the etched glass turned to a cool shade of blue as the tuned symphony of throbbing cylinders settled in, awaiting further instructions. Perhaps at this point I should digress.

My wheels-of-the-week, currently a 2004 Aston Martin DB9, represent what is known as a perk in this town. It just so happens that one of my more grateful clients is a repo man—that is, a repossession agent whose job entails the retrieval of collateral or outstanding leased objects, which, in this case, amounted to the seizure of exotic sports cars, mainly from laid-off dot-com executives out of Silicon Valley and Biotech executives down in San Diego. This particular client began having difficulties with feelings of guilt, remorse, and issues of bad conscience that had escalated to a level where he, himself, was becoming depressed and to the point that it began to interfere with his work. Apparently, he was sensitized by the profusion of sad stories he encountered on a daily basis: the agonies of failed expectations, the cruelty and randomness of fate, and the resulting anguish of his fellow man. In reality, he was simply a nice guy, neither neurotic nor crazy, whose personal sympathies had allowed him to become helplessly mired in the existential anguish and despair of the financial highfliers. By the time he was referred to me for philosophical counseling, he had worked himself up to a point of self-loathing that was becoming a grave concern to his employers.

Guilt, by itself, is neither good nor bad. Like all other emotions, guilt undoubtedly played a significant role in the evolution of human beings and our organized societies. The experience of guilt may have served as a check on wantonness, waste, excessive sexual aggression, and/or flagrant exploitation. In this manner, the avoidance of guilt complements feelings of shame in fostering a sense of social responsibility, without which people might have been more apt to lose their emergent sense of morality and ethics. For better or for worse, guilt hangs heavy on the human mind, often stimulating a great deal of thought, a cognitive preoccupation with some particular wrongdoing, the dubious finding of fault within ourselves, or the development of convoluted schemes for setting things right.

Having first discerned that the client was experiencing an authentic, philosophically accessible form of guilt—as opposed to a neurotic childhood guilt that provokes anxiety or a tacit "guiltiness" in any legal sense—my attention was focused on the moral, ethical, and social aspects of this postmodern dilemma.

Not intending to diminish the phenomenology or subjective experience of guilt, and thus its creative possibilities, I reluctantly accepted the case of the remorseful repo man as a referral. The first stages of my philosophical counseling began with readings and discussions of some pertinent existentialists, namely, Friedrich Nietzsche and Albert Camus. We explored Nietzsche for his critical thoughts concerning the genealogy of morals, the historic origins of *bad conscience*, and the life-enhancing quest for freedom, as viewed from the perspective of a highly rational and self-determined philosopher. With this foundation, we considered the general absurdity of many of man's dilemmas, as voiced by Camus, to gain an appreciation of *the absurdity of life* and our propensity to search for meaning where none can be found.

However, the real breakthrough in the case of the remorseful repo man came when I introduced Mister Nice Guy to the Greek Stoic philosopher, Epictetus, for a discourse on the *true nature of things*, which is invariable and valid for all human beings without exceptions. In terms of clinical philosophy, we partitioned the *nature of things* into two categories: those things that are subject to our exclusive power and those things that are not. The first category includes judgment, impulse, and desire, while the second category includes health, material wealth, fame, and fortune. Next, I introduced the concept of *Prohairesis* (literally, *choice*), the faculty able to use and understand impressions and to render judgment (which is a prime function of Prohairesis).

For the Greeks, Prohairesis is something that distinguishes humans from all other creatures, and it is that to which all other human faculties are subordinated. It is this faculty that, acting in accordance with our own judgments, makes us desirous or aversive, compelled or repelled, assenting-to or dissenting-from anything and everything under the sun. Moreover, it is the very act of judgment performed by our faculty of Prohairesis that is able to distinguish the things contained within the first category (things within our power) from the things relegated to the latter. Each of us exists in our own implicit reality, where we are not only influenced but defined and bounded by the very judgments we make. Once the remorseful repo man thoroughly grasped these concepts and began to employ them in his life and his work, he began to experience an undisturbed and serene state of mind, which is among the most tangible fruits of applied philosophical practice.

In no time at all, the once-remorseful repo man was virtually freed from his responses to all the external objects of our lives, freed from the burdens of their costly acquisition or their loss—freed from the problematic considerations that economic vagaries and vicissitudes are, in any way, up to him or within his power to abate. In fact, this newfound Stoic serenity was contagious to the extent that the benefits of reasoning in accordance with the *true nature of things* ultimately extended to the mournful deadbeats who—after talking at length with the newly inspired repo man—were actually relieved to have him take these earthly burdens off their hands. In no time at all, he became the most successful and the most popular repo man in all of California. And in appreciation for my unique and highly personalized services, I am routinely provided with a slightly used but highly serviceable automobile to run around town for a week or so, before it is formally returned to the creditors. This week, the latest installment just happened to be an Aston Martin DB9 coupe.

Traffic was light, so I cruised down the variegated "Strip" of Sunset Boulevard all the way to the Beverly Hills Hotel, where I turned right onto Crescent Drive. Motoring up the hill, the rows of stately palm trees were replaced by rows of stately pine trees, and the mansions rose to new heights of Italian Renaissance grandeur. There, at the very top of the crescent, just before the road bends to the left and heads back down the hill, stood a Venetian palazzo commanding attention like Cecil B. DeMille himself decked out in full director's regalia. I knew right away without even checking the number that this was the place, so I turned the DB9 into the driveway and turned off the throbbing symphony with a decisive push of the glass button. I have to admit—it is somewhat hard to bear the silence and the stillness that comes with the loss of the visceral ambiance and glove-like embrace of such a finely tuned sports car. And it doesn't help that the "swan wing" doors swing gracefully outward and upward at a twelve-degree angle as one departs, opening up with a demure elegance of form and function that is more reminiscent of a classical ballerina than a mechanical driving machine. I actually had to steel myself to resist the temptation to take her for another spin around the ruins. After all, a Perspicuous Eye is nothing if not professional.

Waiting at the grand entrance, I was half-expecting to be greeted by a servant dressed in a butler's uniform. Instead, Zero Vaynilovich himself opened the door. I have to give him that.

"Joe Metropolis. Good. I was beginning to think I might have scared you off." Standing there in the oversized entranceway, he looked every inch the famous Hollywood writer/director/producer if there ever was one; in fact, there have been many more than one. And there in the blinding arc light of the oversized security lamps, Zero Vaynilovich appeared for a brief moment to embody some if not all of the charismatic qualities of a motion picture tycoon in full command of his realm. Then, just as transitory, a dark shadow of gloom and uncertainty spread across his face as he stepped back into the foyer of his palazzo. "Come on in, Metropolis. We've got work to do."

The scenery inside the villa was distinctly darker, since low-key lighting was obviously still in vogue, creating an atmosphere that accentuates the contours of every visible object, throwing large areas into an impenetrable shade, creating vast sweeping shadows that sliced the vast interior spaces into swaths of blackness that collected in thick pools. Key lights were employed rather sparingly, apparently to create a chiaroscuro effect, like a Rembrandt painting that obscures more than it reveals, thereby heightening both the drama of the occasion and the sense of alienation felt by a visitor. The virtual absence of fill light in the grand living and dining rooms added to the feeling of cavernous darkness and mystery. One must imagine being led through a series of passageways with a single lighted candle to gain a full appreciation of the somber *mise-en-scène* leading to the immense two-story rotunda set within the stylistically darkened hollow of the Zilch residence.

"Take a seat over there," he said as he directed me to a large velvet chair. Then he situated himself in the shadows by leaning against the ornate marble statuary of a gigantic old-world fireplace that was otherwise empty and dark.

"Couldn't we use a little more light, Mister Zilch? I can barely see my own hands."

"What you can or cannot see does not concern me in the least. It is what *I* can see that is of vital importance."

"Okay, Mister Zilch, if you say so. But wouldn't it be more helpful for the both of us if we could see each other more clearly during our conversation? In my experience, direct observation can be most enlightening."

"Forget it, Metropolis. I don't want you to bring some blasted enlightenment into my life. I want you to help me to see more clearly in the dark!"

I began to stand up, with the intention of leaving, when I hesitated. I had detected a brief but discernable note of sincerity in the voice of the shadowy man named Zilch, and I decided to play along.

"Calm down, Metropolis. You're tougher than that. I know that you are, or I wouldn't have hired you. And besides, it's just the way I am. It has nothing to do with you. So don't be offended. And don't expect my manners to improve. I don't have time to be circumspect, you see. My time is running out."

"Okay, Mister Zilch, it's your problem, and it's your nickel. So how do you suggest we proceed?"

"I'll talk, you listen ... just listen. Listen to my words as they're spoken to you. Listen to the words as they come. You can even close your eyes if you like—I won't be offended. You're just another audience out there in the dark, an audience that has become accustomed to taking in impressions solely by the eye and has lost the art of listening carefully. Believe me, I know. I'm in the business of providing the eye candy. But long before there were movies, there were words, there were ideas. Before there were movies, there were dreams of beauty. And this is what I want to tell you about."

Amazing. Here I was, seated in a dark theater ready to offer the services of my highly trained perspicuous eye, when I am being told to close my eyes and "listen." Just like Nietzsche in his preface to *Ecce Homo*: "*Listen! For I am such and such a person. For Heaven's sake do not confound me with anyone else!*" Here was Zero Vaynilovich, movie mogul extraordinaire, attempting to reveal himself to me in the quaint manner of an old-fashioned storyteller. I adjusted myself in the plush velvet chair, and as I did so, Zilch paused momentarily in his discourse.

"Please continue," I said, with an inclination that this might actually be good.

"Recall the oral traditions, the legends, the prophets, the minstrels, the poets. Without even one look, they could break your heart. Without one look, they wrote every part. Their words could make a sad heart sing. Without a single look, you would know all you'd ever need to know."

As he spoke, he began to move around the rotunda, passing through the shadows and the focused spotlights that reflected here on a Greco-Roman statue, there on the gilded frame of an obscure masterpiece, and there on an empty vase as big as the Ritz. It was as if a specter of antiquity were passing by in the darkness and returning again to the vacuous yet finely ornamented hearth, the primal podium of the most ancient of orators.

"There are thoughts that put seventy-millimeter film to shame, thoughts that set the whole world aflame. You know I'm right when it's transcribed in black-and-white—you can look away and still hear what I say." Clearly resisting the impulse to break into song, Zilch continued to drive his point home in a low *sotto voce*. "Yes, without one look, we record our past. Without one look, we make things that last. When we listen in the dark, it's all still out there in the dark."

I was beginning to like this Zilch character. Besides his feigned pomposity with its crusty, hard-boiled exterior enameled by the glaze and gloss that is Hollywood was a note of nostalgia, a melodious hint of irony, and even an aching echo of remorse.

"You see, Metropolis, the story of my life began when I met her. I was in film school, immersed in my studies of basic cinematography, production design, and the craft of filmmaking, completely immersed in, and fairly comfortable with, my own world view seen at twenty-four frames per second. I had just completed my Masters of Fine Arts in film production and direction when I first met her. I was sitting in on a lecture on advanced screenwriting, and she was arguing with a visiting professor about things that were so far over my head that I couldn't follow or even imagine I ever could. It was like, *what star did she fall from to land on this planet?*"

My eyes were beginning to adjust to the low levels of illumination, and I found myself searching for the facial expressions that would betray the subtlety of his true feelings, much to the detriment of his practiced facade. Perhaps Zilch noticed the drift in my attention, for he moved from the carved mantle of the fireplace to a flanking position in the shadows, and then he continued talking, a disembodied voice-over that moved slowly around the dimly lit rotunda.

"I don't know how I managed it—I do know that I wanted it more than anything—but I managed to join in the dialogue from an aspiring director's point of view with just enough substance and confidence for her to notice me. It didn't help that she was sleeping with the famous professor who proctored the screenwriting course and that I was just another celluloid protégé who struts and frets his hour-and-a-half upon the silver screen, just another idiot full of cinematic surround sound and fury, signifying nothing. But I tell you, when she cast her wondrous spell on me, I felt for the first time in my life that everything was possible, that I could be more than a promising young director, that I could achieve something lasting and artistically profound. By aspiring to her level, I could fathom the mystery of creativity itself and harness the power of the imagination."

At this point in the story, I interjected with a narrative hunch. "May I assume that this inspiring woman is Kaltrina Dahl?" Everyone in Hollywood was well aware of the purposeful existence and general appearance of this elusive "Blue Dahlia." Everyone from bit players and paparazzi to auteurs and emcees were acutely aware that her very footsteps were marked with cinematic epiphany.

"That, you may. What you may not know, however, is that everything that I have accomplished, everything that I am, is the result of her inspiration. It was through her admiration that I found the sublime grandeur of literature; through her aspiration, I found my authentic voice as a writer; through her enthusiasm, I found my passion for the stories that give life its form, the stories behind the award-winning cinematic scenes. But it wasn't as simple as it might sound, Metropolis. At first, she was completely unattainable. She was more than aloof; she was utterly out of reach. She was my unreachable, unattainable Blue Dahlia.

"But reach for her, I did," he said, his tone rising. "And believe you me, it was like reaching for the stars. And then, one day, she recognized me as an embryonic artist with potential. It wasn't as if I actually changed in any intellectual or psychological way. It was like she saw something interesting in me—more like she saw a possibility of something interesting within me—and out of this unformed amalgamation of sheer possibility, she created an illustrious image of me. Eventually, I began to see myself in her eyes, to see myself as she saw me, and I liked what I saw.

"Perhaps it was her expectation of my potential preeminence that provided the artistic leaven. I really don't know. But I began to gain some kind of control of the imperatives imbedded within the humanities, control of the intrinsic power of the metaphors that are true to life. With her acute sense of *humanitas* and a renewed appreciation of drama in my mind, the cameras became extensions of my eyes; the passing frames of exposed film became my memories. For the first time, I could examine every scene *a priori*, like the discrete facets of a diamond that I could hold within my brain and gracefully turn within my imagination … until, at last, I found that one angle, that one focus, that one tone that shone with a compelling and wholly original gleam. With the Blue Dahlia's acute sensibilities as my guide, I developed my own original sense of style. Wielding a firebrand from the primordial campfire, the wonder, the imagery, the dialogue, the music, the editing all fell perfectly into place. But it was *she* who was the flame within the fire; it was *she* who was the lamplight behind the lens. Together, we became more powerful and achieved more together than either of us could ever have achieved alone.

"But she was no mere muse; believe me." Now he paced again. Moving slowly around the room, he would pass into the light for the briefest of moments and then disappear again into the shadows. "She was not some kind of gentle nurturer of the artistic soul. More often than not, it was Dahlia who performed the artistic heavy lifting. She didn't just inspire me; it was never that easy. Actually, she was a strident feminist of the first rank, and a fiercely combative mentality at that. If she was some kind of muse, she was certainly a postmodern one. Our partnership was demanding of a perfection that is all too rare, but somehow it was achievable. Our love was an emersion and an ambitious fervor in pursuit of excellence.

"While she was certainly beautiful enough to stand in front of the camera, she was a reluctant exhibitionist, and she remained out of the limelight by her own choice. And yet she was always present in the medium, like a ghost in the machine. She was always there when there was anything of real quality to behold. She was not easy to please but—I can tell you this—when she was pleased, there was nothing like it, anywhere, anytime. There was nothing like it in this world."

He paused there in the darkness, a darkness that had grown steadily, by the days, by the weeks, by the months, until it had blotted out everything else but the pain and the doom. I could hear the telling sound of his breathing there in the darkness, each remorseful sigh an issuance of regret, filled with loss and longing and tender moments of remembrance.

"Our relationship was a copulation of body and soul. When she breathed into my mouth, she infused not only the extreme fullness of her feminine beauty, but her overarching ideals of the perfectibility of man. The nakedness of her revelations became the very breath within my lungs, the straining sinews of the heart of the artist that I was more firmly becoming. And I don't need to tell you, but just being with her was one long awe-inspiring, eye-popping, mind-expanding, breathtaking, death-defying, earth-quaking, timber-shivering orgasm. The Blue Dahlia, like art and life itself, was no longer unattainable. She was blood red, she was astonishingly hot, and she was mine.

"Did I tell you she has the body of a goddess?"

"You didn't have to," I spoke into the darkness, which takes some getting used to. Zero Vaynilovich continued to move about the shadowy rotunda as if he were still searching for something deep within himself.

"But that was only the beginning. The dreams that came with my Dahlia by my side were nothing less than Apollonian exaltations, a light-filled space in which a man like me can enjoy *the immediate apprehension of form* with godlike clarity. In such dreams, a man is healed and helped by receiving an endless array of divine intuitions. In such dreams, a dreamer can immediately grasp the symbols and metaphors of cinematic 'appearances' that are not real in the physical sense, but visionary 'apprehensions' whose cinematic interpretations can lead to artistic truth. With such dreams as source materials, the lucid dreamer returns to the ancient cave where all of life passes before him—not like mere lights and shadows on the wall but like scenes one lives and suffers through, suffers through with a measured restraint of that fleeting sensation of 'appearances' coupled with a director's appreciation of the reality that lies beneath. Needless to say, the applications in terms of moviemaking were quite poignant. Everything turned to gold. I became a high priest of Hollywood. My career blossomed, and you know the rest. The rest is history. Together, we made history, and I got rich and famous. Every man wanted to be my friend, and every woman wanted to have my child. I was living the good life in the radiance of her approval, in the eloquence of her desire.

"And waking up next to her was bliss itself. Our orange juice was fresh squeezed between the thighs of a hundred vestal virgins. Our champagne was made from grapes pressed by Dionysus himself. You can be sure that the Columbian beans for our morning coffee were handpicked and smuggled across the border by none other than Juan Valdez. With my beautiful Blue Dahlia by my side, I was Michelangelo looking down from the ceiling of the Sistine Chapel. I was pointing my own finger in the very vaults of Heaven.

"With the ineffable encouragement that becomes a man when he takes it upon himself to please a woman, I became a self-proclaimed motion picture *artiste*, a quintessential self-made man. Like the figurative diamond that I had learned to turn within my mind—I became hard. I made cinematic history with every movie reel. I became a Hyperborean."

"Hyperborean?" I queried.

"The race of mythical people who live beyond the north wind."

"I see."

"I began to enjoy the supreme confidence of my own genius," he explained. "Then one day, those beautiful eyes blinked, that lovely voice faltered. It was almost imperceptible at first, but then it began to spiral out of control, out of reach, out of sight ... and then she was gone.

"I tried and tried to focus on my work, on my art. Yes, of course, to win her back, to impress her as I once had in the past, as I had when everything was new, when everything really mattered. But more importantly, I had to prove to myself that I could do it alone, as though I always could. But the more I tried, the less and less I succeeded." Zilch continued to pace the floor, moving in and out of the shadows with increasing rapidity. "Sure, sure, the wheels of Tinseltown still turned for me, doors were opened, actors and actresses swooned, rose petals and jacaranda blossoms were strewn at my feet, but I could always tell that I had lost my edge. The more I tried to recapture that creative spark, the more derivative my films became, the more stylistic, the more extravagant, the more degenerate, the more lewd, the more violent. The further I fell from artistic grace, the more I had to rely on spectacle and the more grotesque it all became until, at last—damn it all—there were nothing but sequels to show for myself. In the end, and I tell you I am nearing the end, my movies have become, for me, a museum—a museum unto myself." Then he poured himself into a velvet chair, covering his face with his hands.

I was dumfounded. Here, in the presence of this self-proclaimed museum of a man, I was indeed beginning to see—to see, as it were—in the dark. I was beginning to see with some salient philosophical insights into the character and the conundrum of the man named Zilch. Yet this sense of dark tragedy might not have seen the light of day without the direct metaphorical reference to Apollo, the god of beauty in appearance, the god of plastic arts and of illusion, the god of every plastic form. Of course, isn't it clear? Cinema is the penultimate *Plastic Art*—a superficial world of appearances without anything actually appearing—a world in which truth itself is continuously replaced by the beauteous appearance of a dream world, an appearance of an appearance.

Yes, indeed, the motion picture industry is a microcosm that champions the Apollonian *principium individuationis*, the principle that both exalts the individual and establishes the boundaries that separate men and women from the real world and from each other. That bit about the dreamer as the perfect artist was, for me, a dead giveaway. However, we also know from an application of pertinent mythology and philosophy that Apollo himself plays only a mediating role here and that the primacy in the creative process belongs to Dionysus, the god of immersion and intoxication and ecstatic emotions who is the "true being" and the "true originator." Moreover, when the Apollonian boundaries begin to break down, when darkness and dissolution of the individual ensues, you can be sure that Dionysus is not far off.

"I think I follow you, Mister Zilch, and perhaps I can help you in some way. Speaking in the theatrical, if not cinematic terms of Arthur Schopenhauer, the definitive criterion of philosophical ability is the gift of regarding man and things as mere phantoms and dream-pictures. The only problem I have with your story is the modern existentialist's assumption that any experience that is intelligible—as you have strived very intelligibly to present your experiences to me here this evening—is already an illusion, answering to nothing in the real world itself."

"Are you calling me a liar, Metropolis? Because if you are …"

"No. Not a liar in the pejorative sense, but an artistic creator by nature."

"Then say what you mean, dammit! This is hard enough for me as it is."

"What I mean to say is that our private world, as we see it, is necessarily perceived somewhat creatively, as it streams through the 'primal faculty' of the human imagination like a fiery liquid. That is, it is only by conveniently forgetting that we ourselves are constantly, artistically creating subjects—and perhaps even *lost objects*—that we can live with any sense of security and consistency."

"It still sounds to me that you don't believe me at all," said Zilch with noticeable disappointment.

"On the contrary, I'm listening very carefully, like you asked me to, and I'm simply trying to consider the possibility that there may be more than one side to this story."

"I try to tell you my story, from my own point of view, and you go and criticize me for telling you my own story. If this is philosophy, you can keep it. Actually, Metropolis, I don't want any part of it—never did. And if you want to know the truth, I have absolutely no faith in philosophy whatsoever." As he spoke, he rose to his feet and gazed anxiously about the room, as if he were looking for an EXIT sign. Then he turned abruptly back around and spoke in my direction. "But *she* does! And at one point in time, Kaltrina read your book, and she confided in me how much she admired your damned insights. And that's why I'm standing here in the dark, being all so conscientiousness and all and allowing you to criticize me in my own house, under my own roof."

"Calm down, Mister Zilch. You're tougher than that. I know you are, or I wouldn't have critiqued your storytelling. And besides, it's just the way of the world. It has nothing to do with you."

"All right, all right, Metropolis, you win. I'll try not to be offended. And I don't need an echo in my own palazzo to tell me that my time is running out."

"Fair enough, I won't repeat the obvious. But I am kind of curious as to the nature of the stolen object you mentioned previously. It could help me with my inquiries on your behalf."

"Forget it, Metropolis. I've told you too much already," he said abruptly. "You just find out *why* my Dahlia left me—the real reason—and you can leave the rest to me."

Taking this as a cue for me to rise from the comfort of the plush velvet chair, I pressed the issue, saying, "Is it safe to assume, then, that you know exactly where she is?"

"Not quite. It's much too painful for me to endure all the emasculating details concerning who, what, when, and where, but I do have people in my employ that can provide you with such information on a need-to-know basis."

"And how, then, do you suggest we proceed?"

"You start by having lunch tomorrow at the Café Med on Sunset."

3. The Loneliest Number

The Café Mediterranean is a popular hangout for the up-and-coming who "do lunch" on the sidewalks of the Sunset Plaza in West Hollywood. With curbside tables comfortably ensconced under an olive green awning that curves around the street corner, the trendy Italian restaurant is a prime location for viewing an occasional celebrity on parade in the midst of the endless streams of wide-eyed tourists, stylish fashionistas, and supermodel wannabes on cruise patrol up and down the hallowed pavements of the Sunset Strip. As the Aston Martin DB9 coupe rounded the corner like a deft chariot and nosed into a parking space in the lot behind the café, I could smell the aromas of *pappardelle al telefono* and the *pizza montecarlo* wafting delectably through the air.

It was pretty early for lunch, even by Southern California standards, so I had no trouble getting a table with a prominent view of the street scene. No one in particular appeared to be looking for me, outside of the usual nonchalant evaluations of everyone by everyone else in order to ascertain whether somebody was anybody of importance, followed by the customary disdain accorded to anyone who turns out to be no one in particular. And so, after passing an acceptable amount of waiting time sipping an espresso macchiato and some sparkling water in the shade of the Solisequious Strip, I was able to enjoy the *tortino di melanzane alla parmigiana*, the savory special of the day, in the comfort of my own relative anonymity, which is not always the case.

I was beginning to wonder when the anticipated private detective would eventually arrive to get this show on the road. After all, Zero Vaynilovich is not a man you would want to disappoint, not if you ever wanted to "do lunch" again in this town. Just then, a young man who appeared to be a recent émigré from south of the border wearing an LA Angels baseball jersey and brandishing a handful of Star Maps crossed the street and approached my table directly from the sidewalk.

"Hey, Señor, you want to buy a Star Map." Curiously, he sounded somewhat more didactic than interrogatory.

"Thank you, but I'm not quite sure," I said enigmatically, as I found myself gazing at my own distorted image in the mirrored lenses of his aviator sunglasses.

"I'm sure, Señor. You want to buy this Star Map."

"Okay, I get it," I said as I reached for my wallet and handed the young man a twenty. Even a highly trained *perspicuous eye* can be slow to adjust to the glare of broad daylight.

The cover of the Star Map looked ordinary enough: "List of Movie Stars' Homes, plus Sightseeing, Walk of Fame, Entertainment, and Discount Coupons," along with an assuring notice, "Revised Every 90 Days." There among the colorfully illustrated maps of celebrities' homes and the locations of eventful happenings, a circle was drawn by hand around a portion of Mulholland Drive, and within that circle was printed the name of the well-known writer, Byron Harmsway, along with what turned out to be his unlisted phone number. I glanced up again and looked around, but the messenger with the Star Maps was nowhere in sight.

I skillfully thumbed the designated numbers onto my cell phone with one hand as I savored the last sips of my third espresso macchiato with the other and signaled the waitress with a nod—such is the skill set of the postmodern man about town.

"Hello. If you have dialed this number, you already know with whom you would like to speak. We are exercising our right of privacy at this time. Please hang up or leave a message and then wait patiently by the phone until we decide whether or not to call you back." The recorded message was delivered by the sultry voice of an overly evocative machine.

"Hello. My name is Joe Metropolis, and I would like to talk with Mister Byron Harmsway about Kaltrina Dahl. In the event that such conversation is deemed suitable, you may reach me anon by return call." Two can play at the game of sardonic civility.

By the time I paid the check, the classical insinuations of my cell phone ringtone were already informing me of the return call.

"Hello. Metropolis here," I said reflexively.

The voice on the other end of the electromagnetic waveform was that of a male who spoke softly with perfect diction and a noticeable lilt, like a summer breeze through a set of wind chimes.

"I am Mister Harmsway's personal assistant. Can you come right away?"

"I'll be there in about thirty minutes," I said, mentally plotting my course along Coldwater Canyon, rather than the congested Sunset Plaza Drive route over Lookout Mountain, in a manner more befitting good digestion and the general temperament of the Aston Martin DB9 coupe.

. . .

There's no doubt about it—it is better to travel well than to arrive. Particularly if the traveling well is brought to a screeching halt at a gated entrance and the arrival amounts to a painfully slow procession through a narrow passage flanked by parched earthen berms leading down a single-lane driveway behind a slow-walking security guard who trudges wearily along the circuitous path like a mule around a grindstone, eventually coming upon a setting that offends the eye with an obscene display of wealth, bad taste, and leisure living so typical of a So Cal multimillion-dollar manse.

I was greeted at the grand entrance of the chateau by a rather delicate man in a lavender satin shirt that matched his soft wind-chime voice.

"Doctor Metropolis, I presume?" Spoken like I had just come from some dark continent far away. "I'm so glad you're here. He's cleaning his gun again, and I am afraid that something terrible is going to happen."

"I see," I said, entering into the archaic opulence of a minstrel's gallery that served as the front entrance to this hillside chateau. I didn't figure my soft-spoken guide needed to know that I was there for another client. And besides, while I was on the case, I figured I'd see what I could do for his boss.

With Wind Chimes leading the way on what appeared to be his tiptoes, I traversed a great room with oversized windows and ceilings high enough to create their own weather patterns and passed through the conservatory, where filtered sunlight streamed in tenuous fingers and the sweet smells of jasmine and honeysuckle drifted in through the screened windows of an adjacent sunroom. The far end of the conservatory opened into a handsome library with a crystal chandelier and floor-to-ceiling shelves of books spanning three walls. The furthest wall was occupied by an expansive bow window that looked out over manicured gardens and a built-in bar that was stocked as orderly, and as fully, as the bookshelves.

Byron Harmsway did not get up when I entered the library. His masculine frame—at times well muscled for his various roles, though not so now—was bent over the desk, a wisp of soft, gray-brown hair falling into his recognizable, sharply defined brow. Before him, the minimalist mechanical parts of an antique handgun were sprawled upon the leather surface of a mahogany partner's desk. I watched Harmsway as he continued to reassemble the gun. This man, who had for so long captured the hearts of many female Hollywood enthusiasts, was beginning to show signs of age.

"Doctor Metropolis is here to see you, Byron. Please be so kind as to give him your full attention."

Without a word, Byron Harmsway completed the assembly and began placing six bullets, one by one, into the empty cylinders of the revolver. He flipped the loading gate closed, thumbed the hammer to half cock, and spun the cylinder.

"Well now, that's enough of that," he said as he lowered the barrel of the pistol to a firing position and aimed its muzzle directly at my chest. "If I've learned anything about human nature in my travels around the world it is this: when you need a proper weapon, you need it badly—you should always keep it handy, and you should always keep it loaded. You see, a handgun, like a human being, like nature itself, abhors a vacuum."

"It's not what goes into the empty chambers of the human psyche that concerns me, Mister Harmsway; it's *what* and, more importantly, *when* and *where* that something loaded within those empty chambers decides to come out."

"Finally, a philosopher with balls!" he exclaimed as he waved the firearm casually about. Then he pointed the barrel upward, drawing the cylinder of the revolver very close to his ear, as if he were listening—listening in the silence for a motive that would dispel the world's anxieties, listening for the classical mechanics that move the atoms and the stars, listening for the assurance of a solid mechanistic sound as he slowly, purposefully, conclusively uncocked the hammer. Then he placed the weapon back on the desk in front of him.

"She sent you to help me, didn't she?" he asked me, somewhat rhetorically.

"If you mean Kaltrina Dahl, then no. I've never met her."

"Who sent you then? Who the hell sent Joe freaking Metropolis to help little old me?"

"I'm not at liberty to divulge that information, Mister Harmsway."

"Why the hell not?"

"It's a matter of professional ethics, Mister Harmsway. As you know, confidentiality is of paramount importance to both a Philosophical Counselor and his client, particularly when they endeavor to explore the darkest recesses of the human mind and to discuss the most intimate details of troublesome and aberrant modes of thinking."

"I hear the words," said the man—once filled with confidence and prepossessing authority, but no longer—as he stared down at the loaded revolver. It was almost as if he were struggling to resist the urge to perform another mechanical maintenance operation right then and there. Finally, with considerable effort and fortitude, he looked up again, and his face brightened. "I can appreciate your position, Joe. As a journalist and a war correspondent—that is, before I came to Hollywood—I used those same words to cover my ass and my sources. Nevertheless, it doesn't seem right that you should miraculously appear out of nowhere at a time like this. It doesn't seem right that someone is in charge and I can't know who it is—that you get to know all about me while I am left completely in the dark. That just doesn't seem fair, does it?"

"Is that a philosophical question?" I asked, attempting to break the ice.

"Indeed it is. Indeed it is," he said again as he signaled for Wind Chimes to leave the room with a wave of his calloused hand. "Sit down and make yourself comfortable, Joe. You're making me nervous. And call me Byron, for Pete's sake. After all, we're both on the same side of the typewriter."

He offered me a drink, which I courteously declined, stating that I was serving as my own designated driver today. Nonetheless, he proceeded to pour a considerable amount of whiskey from a monogrammed decanter into two fluted shot glasses on the bar, a process that was soon to be familiar, as it was repeated several times.

"I'm here to find out something unique and interesting about Kaltrina Dahl, Byron, and I have reason to believe that you might be able to help me."

"You think that *I* can help *you* with Kaltrina? You've got to be kidding."

"Well, I have to admit that my instructions do appear to be rather vague."

"That woman damn near ruined my life!" He went on to tell me all about *having* something marvelous and exotic and romantic and then *not having it* in great detail. From what I could gather, Kaltrina nursed him back to health after he was seriously wounded in the Gulf War. Apparently, he was shot in parts unknown and was never quite the same. It was as if a part of him died there. Like he felt his own soul or something like it coming right out of his body—like you'd pull a silk handkerchief out of a pocket by one corner—and it flew all around and then came back and went in again; it wasn't exactly dead, but it wasn't exactly folded the same way that it was before he was shot in parts unknown.

Before the onset of the crisis, his life had been running smoothly enough. He was as happy and content as any person who had already realized many of his life's ambitions. Prior to the onset of the crisis, everything had been going extremely well for Byron. He had become a world-famous journalist, war correspondent, and writer of fiction whose documentaries and novels had been made into Hollywood movies. Prior to the onset of the crisis, he was able to immerse himself fully in the pursuit of happiness, wealth, and recognition. He was living the so-called good life, building a larger-than-life persona, and reveling in the plentitude of the American Dream, when the randomness of fate spread out like a dark shadow upon the shifting sands of a particular desert storm, when a mortar round found him passing out cigarettes and refrigerated chocolates to actual soldiers. Suddenly, the self-proclaimed realist who characteristically wrote about bloodshed and action found out for himself what bloodshed and action is all about.

It turns out that some wounds heal while others do not. Oh, yes, Byron's flesh wounds healed well enough, but then strange things began to happen within him. He was often overcome with extended periods of creeping perplexity that led eventually to a complete arrest of life, as though he no longer knew how to live or what to do, and he became increasingly lost and dejected and intensely unhappy. His personal crisis was characterized by an acute sense of the complete meaninglessness of all his favorite activities and previous achievements. He could no longer find either meaning or purpose in writing or camping or hunting or fishing or even bullshitting with the guys and gals. At this point, Byron refilled his whiskey glasses again and tilted them back, one by one, as he carried on in this two-fisted manner. Whether he liked it or not, there was nothing he could do to prevent or ignore the mounting unhappiness of his existential despair. He was becoming powerless to resist the *gravitas* and the relentless pull of the incipient meaninglessness.

At this pre-reflective point in the story, it would be opportune for a conscientious Philosophical Counselor to remind such a client that many intelligent and highly accomplished intellectuals have become shipwrecked upon these very same shoals. Indeed, there are many among these hapless individualists who view philosophical inquiry concerning the meaning of human existence as pointless, superfluous questioning that can actually interfere with what they assume to be the real meaning of existence. Enamored with their own heroic brand of suffering, the question of the meaning of existence is often considered to be nothing but a distraction. But then, the purposeful questioning of our assumptions is the very essence of philosophy.

It occurred to me that Byron Harmsway could have benefited enormously from an exercise in Applied Philosophy that was aimed at confronting the emptiness and meaninglessness that overcame him rather than allowing it to propel him into a state of anxiety, negation, and despair from which there is no recovery. The philosophical exercise that came to mind was that of questioning the whole of our modern assumptions, including the limitations of scientific thinking, with its tedious incremental methods, and the value of rational thought, with its stilted claims to be the source of all knowledge. For one to take control of the constructive process of philosophical questioning is to take the bull by the horns, so to speak; and any matador who is able to face down the primal ferocity of his own existential meaninglessness with such poise and aplomb is, in my perspicuous view, truly heroic. The ability to question the very meaning of existence within the context of a ripsnorting perplexity can serve to provide a panoramic view of the blood red tapestry of human behavior within the grand spectacle of life and death.

Meanwhile, it would take a special kind of nursing to restore a confidence so badly damaged, to coax the man's flagging vigorousness back to life, to assuage the persistent insomnia of someone who has suddenly become terrified of his own *inner dark*. And that particular kind of nursing was apparently provided by none other than Kaltrina Dahl. It was Kaltrina who had respected Byron Harmsway enough to eschew the knee-jerk conclusions that Byron's war wounds had led to unconscious conflicts of which he was largely unaware, conflicts of desire and satisfaction that could only be addressed and resolved by psychoanalytic formulations. After all, Byron Harmsway had managed to achieve what most people in this world can only dream of achieving. Kaltrina Dahl had respected Byron and his wounds enough to see his progressive dis-ease for what it was and to use her feminine powers to draw him back from the abyss and into the world.

Had Byron Harmsway been my client who had come to me at an earlier stage in the progression of his dis-ease, we might have engaged in a scholarly discourse concerning the underlying disillusionment and pathos that assailed many great writers. For Jean-Paul Sartre, the loss of orientation in the world that arises from a direct experience of the senselessness and meaninglessness of existence was described as a form of nausea: *"I feel like vomiting—and all of a sudden, there it is: the Nausea."*[4] For Albert Camus, a universe suddenly divested of illusions and lights, where a man feels alien, without memory of home or sense of hope, becomes the absurd: *"This divorce between man and his life,*

---

4   J-P Sartre in *Nausea*.

the actor and his setting, is properly the feeling of absurdity."[5] For Martin Heidegger, the nausea and absurdity of existence was described as an anxiety, "*An experience of the uncanniness of being.*"[6] And for Friedrich Nietzsche, the experience itself was blacker than death: "*Is not night and more night coming on all the while?*"[7] All these literary accounts describe a condition of dis-ease and despair and a state of being that is so completely detached from the world that is aptly described by Victor Frankl as an "existential vacuum."

But Byron Harmsway did not come to me at an agreeably conversant and, thus, philosophically accessible stage of his dis-ease; rather, in the grips of his own personal nausea, his own unique brand of absurdity and anxiety and gathering darkness, he found his own inscrutable vacuum, and it is into this inscrutable vacuum that Kaltrina Dahl blew Byron Harmsway the most passionate of all kisses—kisses delivered upon the awe-inspiring wings of love.

Apparently, for Kaltrina Dahl, the desperate philosophical malaise of modern man is not a point of departure but an opportunity for feminine intervention, and her preferred form of intervention is overwhelmingly erotic and romantic. Apparently, the meaninglessness of one hand clapping is becoming more and more pertinent in terms of modern feminist theory. Listening carefully to Byron Harmsway weaving the story of his recent psychic restoration into a form of true confession, as I had listened to Zero Vaynilovich tell virtually the same story just the other day, there was no doubt in my mind that Byron had fallen deeply and completely in love with Kaltrina Dahl and that her love for him was similarly transformative. As an artist, his vision expanded; as a thinker, his presuppositions were shattered; as a writer, his creations waxed authentic; as a lover, his exaltation was restored. That is, until she left.

It was becoming clear to me, if not to Byron Harmsway, that a definite pattern was beginning to emerge here. When a man is content and happy with the appurtenances of his own success; when he is basking in the glow of his fame as a brilliant writer/artist/macho man, there is no desperate need for her involvement, her sublime meaning,

---

5   Albert Camus in *The Myth of Sisyphys.*
6   Heidegger in *Being and Time.*
7   Nietzsche in *The Gay Science.*

or her lofty values. In other words, she is no longer needed here—not in this self-satisfied part of town.

And then the unbearable sadness sets in. What was once a source of inspiration and even exaltation becomes a source of misery and angst for the woebegone *artiste*. In one way or another, all great love stories consistently embody great personal tragedies and losses, which can inspire either great art or serious dysphoria, as the individual case may be. In the case of the legendary Kaltrina Dahl, the alluring yet elusive Blue Dahlia, the impassioned evocation aimed at drawing this disillusioned *artiste* back into the world carried with it a touch of the femme fatale.

"It's killing me, Joe. Not knowing anything about life's meaning is hard enough for a man like me, but it can be tolerated. What I can't seem to tolerate is *not knowing* what I did wrong. It was bad enough when the world was at war and I knew what I had to do each day. It was hard enough to face my own uncertainties and my fear of death alone. But now that she has waltzed so exquisitely and so profoundly into my life, I'm lost without her *intimacy*. And the emptiness she left me with is even worse than the meaninglessness I had to endure before she came into my life."

"So if I understand you correctly, you're telling me that your unrequited love of a woman is even more unbearable than the most pressing of philosophical questions?"

"Don't you try to trap me, Joe. Don't you even try. I'll blow your head clean off," he said, once again picking up the handgun and waving it threateningly in my direction.

"I'm not trying to do anything of the kind, Byron. I'm simply trying to reorder our priorities in terms of immediate urgency and necessity," though I was somewhat relieved when he finally put the gun down again. I was all the more relieved when I realized, with full perspicuity, that quite a few of the volumes that graced the walls of Byron's library were riddled with large-caliber bullet holes, particularly the sections that appeared to contain the works of other contemporary authors.

He leaned forward on the desk with the support of his clenched fists, saying, "In that case, it's urgent that you find Kaltrina as soon as possible. And it's urgent that I see her again before it's too late!" The desperation seeped out of him like cold sweat.

"Do you have any idea why she might have left without explaining her reasons?" I was, of course, simply fishing for the obvious in a relatively shallow pool.

"No. But I wish I did. If you ask me, it was a dirty trick. This whole business of love and sex and artistic aspiration is nothing but a dirty trick," he said, looking thoroughly deflated. "One day you get it and you think you're happy, and the next day you wake up and it's all gone and you're alone, and you try to figure out what's missing—like solving some grand deductive equation—but you fail, and then she shows you what's missing and you believe her, because you want to believe her, but you can't believe her, because she's unreliable, and the next day you wake up and you're alone again, and you try to be strong and manly and to live by a code of your own, but you know all along that it was just a trick. Everything is nothing but a lowdown, dirty, rotten, trick."

"Calm down, Byron. Is it really as bad as all that? You know when *eros* and *philos*—that is, erotic love and intellectual attraction—fail to satisfy our emotional needs, the ancient Greeks suggested that we consider a third and higher form of love: *agape*, which seeks nothing in return."

"Oh, balls! You give me concepts while I sing for my supper. Concepts are no good at all for a man in my condition. I pride myself in being a man of action, a man of decisive action. I live by a code I can live with. I keep my weapon handy, clean, and well-oiled, and I strive to keep my mind in a clean, well-lighted place. For me, the shortest answer to any question is just doing the thing. Concepts are no good at all for a man in my condition, Joe." He began to fondle the gun again. "In the beginning, there was nothing but darkness, and then there were concepts of enlightenment, but still there was nothing, only this time, you could see the nothing more clearly in the darkness. It's still nothing, Joe. It's still nothing at all to me."

And that was my signal to leave before I became an inadvertent target for Byron's increasing angst. On my way out, I passed through the conservatory to the great room, where I was greeted again by the sound of Wind Chimes, who approached me on tiptoes.

"Do you think you can help him, Doctor Metropolis?"

"I really don't think so," I said as we arrived at the minstrel's gallery. "From my perspicuous point of view, he is so afraid of the loneliness that he just can't stop replaying a role that turns his victimization cult into a heroic quest with a loaded gun, a bottle of whiskey, and an empty flashlight. He appears to be so afraid of the nothingness that he can't stop hunting it."

"Isn't that somewhat ambiguous, Doctor Metropolis?"

"Yeah, you're right about that. And it's too bad ... because moral ambiguity is my business."

*

On my way back to town, I called Zilch and gave him the scoop in some detail. He listened silently to the whole story, and then, surprisingly, he began to sympathize with his would-be rival.

"Now I almost feel sorry for him," he said. "You know that writers can be insufferably sensitive. Maybe I'll throw the poor sap a bone. Perhaps I'll offer to make a movie out of the worst thing he's ever written. Who knows, it could be a win-win situation."

"And what exactly is the worst thing he's ever written?"

"Why, his latest story entitled, **A Grimy, Dark-Day Over There**, of course." And that was the last thing Zero Vaynilovich said to me before the Great (albeit perennial) Studio Fire that just happened to ignite in the wee hours of the following morning.

• • •

The police were convinced that it was a case of arson/suicide when the badly charred body of Byron Harmsway was found on the floor of one of the burned-out movie sets in the back lot of Cosmopolitan Studios. Even though the coroner reported three distinct bullet wounds in the chest of the dead man, only one of them was considered to be fatal, and so it was an open-and-shut case of arson/suicide. No wonder unsolved murder mysteries are largely a thing of the past in this town.

The next day, I met Zilch, and we strolled through the ashes of the studio back lot as one might stroll through a city park—only the landscapes, lake scenes, and picturesque vistas in this particular park were composed with yards of stage-paint-bedecked upon miles of plywood and lumber that had apparently gone up in flames, along with several decades of Hollywood history, in the early hours of the previous morning. The unmitigated flames had torn through block after block of familiar movie sets, transforming nominative facades and soundstages, idyllic streetscapes and recognizable neighborhoods into the charred and twisted rubble of a disaster movie.

Strolling through the sodden ruins, still smoldering in the noonday sun, we came upon the wasted remains of the massive video vault and film library that had once archived thousands of original films, negatives, and videos, but which now lay sprawled in a great heap of fallen I-beams and girders, revolting only faintly with diminishing plumes of black smoke. There among the thousands of burned and melted videocassettes, among the piles of charred and unspooled movie reels, wafting faintly in the breeze, were the last remains of a vast collection of analog tape, faintly wafting through the universe in a metaphorical dénouement of their last ending.

There was no doubt about it—a change of venue was in the air. With the emergence of digital media, cable TV, digital video, and the evolution of mobile wireless displays, this was a business that had been dying out long before the fire. And since Zilch may have had something to gain from the untimely demise of Byron Harmsway, I couldn't help but wonder. As we stopped to examine the collapsed bricks and strewn pieces of metal that had just yesterday been an exact replica of the Empire State Building, I felt compelled to make my ponderings known.

"You didn't have anything to do with this conflagration, did you, Mister Zilch?"

Zilch kicked aside a pile of jagged glass that lay in our path with the nonchalance of a guy swatting a flea. "Certainly not!" he harrumphed, now moving across the charred backdrops of the set while I followed close behind. "I didn't have to," he added. "All I would have to do is suggest that it might not be such a bad idea, and somehow things like this would manage to happen, and before too long, if not immediately, and definitely within a year or so."

"Somehow I don't find your explanation to be all that comforting."

"Don't worry, Metropolis. We'll build it up again even better than before. Studio sets, as you know, are eternally recurrent!"

We came to the sad ruins of the King Kong attraction, where the giant ape once bellowed at tourists while he tilted the Brooklyn Bridge and the artificial scent of his banana breath was pumped into the air. His defiant torso with its fabulous wooly exterior had been reduced to a carcass of smoldering fur. We crossed over a makeshift police barrier, and I leaned down to stroke the charred remains of the creature.

"It's kind of a shame that the entire King Kong exhibit was totally destroyed in the fire. It was like a shrine for so many around the world. It's almost as if we set him up and then we killed him. The grand majestic primitive King Kong whose power and even his sublime virtues were displayed well enough for all to see, yet his only fault was his being too big, which presented a problem of sheer naturalistic grandiosity and scale."

"Don't worry so much, Metropolis. In his place, we'll erect the image of a new Superman, followed perhaps by a litany of superheroes, all with supernatural powers."

"But isn't that just a bit dubious, Mister Zilch, considering your previously artful and highly cultured motion pictures? Isn't it just a bit onerous, philosophically, to postulate that such virtues and strengths would be derived from supernatural sources?"

"Not just supernatural, but extraterrestrial, my dear philosopher." Zilch spread his arms out wide before him as if he were personally opening the curtains of a Saturday matinee. "Imagine, if you would, that the source of all power and glory, all strength and resolve, would be visited upon our children's children by a fleet of superheroes that have nothing to do with our ways of thinking, our evolutionary history, our various cultures, or even our innate intelligence—having instead been conveniently delivered from afar, like a pepperoni pizza."

"Actually, I can't imagine it, Mister Zilch. It would appear to me to be a form of tragedy." I stifled a sneeze, as the lingering stench of toxic fumes still rising from the ashes of the superannuated movie sets offended my nose and my eyes.

"Oh, that's not the worst of it, Metropolis. It's not just a new superhero bonanza we have here—it doesn't stop there—the suspension of disbelief might even extend to the point where all of man's troubles, all the psychological and sociological ills that afflict mankind, might conceivably have been delivered from outer space."

"I really can't imagine."

"When you combine sheer superstition with a primitive reverence for the random and inscrutable forces of nature—such as a volcano—there is no telling what kinds of absurdities could be brought to bear. You might even go so far as to establish a new cult of religious belief.... Stranger things have happened."

"And you would endorse such foolish thinking, for the sake of entertainment?"

"I don't endorse anything, Metropolis; I just project the pictures on the wall. Without the refinements of my Blue Dahlia to inspire me to greater heights of artistic blossoming, there is always superstition to portray—extravagantly and with visual special effects." As he spoke, we stepped back over the police tape and headed further up the hill to survey the extent of the devastation.

"But, Mister Zilch, doesn't that tend to create an atmosphere wherein all human responsibilities are eroded, if not obviated, where human virtues and responsibilities are provided from afar, doesn't that create an intolerable lightness of being?"

"Oh, come now, Metropolis, don't be so serious. It could be worse. It's not as if the bastions of Western civilization and European decorum, as developed and preserved by the literacy of the British Empire, were reduced to rubble by the hawking of medieval sorcery to unwitting schoolchildren. It's not as if the publishing industry were in cahoots with the motion picture industry to manufacture a plethora of inane bestsellers and blockbusters through the insidious machinations of mass-marketing strategies. It's not as if we all conspire to promote and exploit the black cauldron of witchcraft. You don't actually think that something like that could happen in this day and age, do you?"

"Perhaps not, but I do advocate a certain level of social responsibility in my philosophical practice, and it seems to me that such responsibility would tend to discourage the promotion of ideologies that encourage mass stupidity."

"Oh, you can't blame me for that, Metropolis. Mass stupidity was here long before I came to this town."

4. Superfluous Supermen

Four days later, we bid farewell to the moral ambiguity of Byron Harmsway at the Hollywood Forever Memorial Park. Having spent the better part of the morning in serious contemplation, cruising along the Pacific Coast Highway, winding past the Malibu Hills and Pacific Palisades nestled in sumptuous black leather upholstery, embraced by the carbon fiber chassis of a nearly-new Basalt Black Porsche Carrera GT, I was feeling an array of emotions concordant with the rapid passage of time. It was with some reluctance, yet necessitated by an immediate sense of urgency, that I headed away from the vanishing-edge swimming pool of the Pacific Ocean and started my journey inland toward the gaping maw of an open gravesite and the next scheduled appointment with my client, Zero Vaynilovich. As usual, I was running late.

For the purpose of expediency, I took a portion of California Route 2 that runs from the Santa Monica/Los Angeles city limit as Santa Monica Boulevard, through the exceedingly wealthy habitats of West Los Angeles, Westwood, Century City, and Beverly Hills, passing through the decidedly urban and increasingly commercialized purviews of West Hollywood before entering into a vast and deteriorating streetscape of Hollywood, with its blighted mini-malls, cheesy studios, desolate storage warehouses, pawn shops, automobile chop shops, and other nondescript business enterprises conducted behind painted-over windows and sun-bleached venetian blinds on the sainted street where male and female prostitutes and transgender sex workers ply their notorious trade. Remarkably, this is the very same route that many of the notable celebrities attending Byron Harmsway's rather unceremonial internment service had taken.

I hit the brakes at the Hollywood Forever sign, as the universal symbol for *infinitas* flashed into view, and I turned the Porsche hard right onto Pineland Avenue, where I slowed to a halt beside the small gatehouse. I was directed forward to a waiting fleet of parking attendants. If there is one stratifying theme, one prevailing constant in all of Hollywoodland, it is the sacred tradition of valet parking at any and all occasions.

I handed the overeager parking attendant the valet key, in an effort to ensure that the five-piece set of leather luggage matched exactly to the black leather interior of the Porsche would still be in the trunk when I returned. I followed my assigned usher-lady down the hallowed pavement and onto the VIP section of the star-studded cemetery, where celluloid heroes of ancient starlight lay silently in repose. We passed by the orderly rows of carved headstones, the newer versions of which were turned eerily sideways, beaming with life-size faces laser-etched into the upstanding marble, as if to see who was coming to visit them, to adore them even still. A faint smell of the crematory wafted on the aerial sighs of a midsummer breeze.

I found Zilch standing there among a small group of invited admirers, including men in black polo shirts and sport jackets and women in strapless gowns and sleeveless summer dresses with fashionable black veils. He was munching on a chocolate chip cookie, provided by the Hollywood Forever on-site concierge service that, apparently, also provided the floral tributes and the folding chairs. In addition to the open coffin poised precariously on the threshold of a telltale rectangular pit, I noticed a pair of stainless steel coffee dispensers and two stacks of styrofoam cups on a linen-covered table, and I began pumping away at the House Blend, trying really hard not to notice the cast of a dozen or so lugubrious celebrities in attendance.

"Well, if it isn't Joe Metropolis," said Zero Vaynilovich with a mouthful of chocolate chips. "Now that you're here, we can get this over with."

Faced by a curious gaggle of Hollywood's finest, I found myself at a loss for words. Not so Zilch, for he was in his element. Here at the edge of Byron's eternal resting place, he was the quintessential showman.

"Ladies and gentlemen, as Eric von Stroheim once said, '*In Hollywood, you're only as good as your last picture,*[8] and I believe that to be true for a writer as well. So today it is my great pleasure to inform you that I will be directing the movie adaptation of Byron Harmsway's last story myself, as well as his digital video memorial, which we will begin filming today." Zilch raised his hands to the sky as if he was personally repositioning the planets. The congregation bustled with approval. "As Byron's official multimedia biographer, director, and producer, I will make it my business to see that his video Life Story is the best damn Life Story ever, and that, even in death, he will be larger than life—larger and better than he ever was."

Zilch went on to explain the theme of Byron's "Life Story" in cinematic terms that sounded, in actuality, more like one would describe a modern music video than a formal documentary. I should mention that the production of a digital video memorial is a serious art form that is much in vogue these days, an art form where people are not so much as buried as they are *archived* in the manner of a professionally produced motion picture, in film libraries and dedicated databases, on DVDs available at the cemetery's gift shop, or forever viewable as a rented plot of cyberspace on the Internet. Still, I couldn't help but notice that Zilch's *treatment* of Byron's digital Life Story was to be linked in the storyboard to his last novel and that it sounded more like the coming attractions for an unmade movie than any kind of memorial service I had ever heard or seen before.

"Byron himself is going to make a cameo appearance in my next film, and that's all I can say at this time." And then it was over—the memorial service, that is—and the preparations for the director's cut began.

In no time at all, movie-making equipment began to roll out of nowhere onto the cemetery lawn: dollies, tracks, video cranes, booms, lights, reflectors, and steady-cams appeared with their operators who mingled among the designated celebrities along with a bevy of technicians of every conceivable specialty. Like a school of fish that moves curiously, purposefully *en masse*, responding to some presumed but not easily discernable stimulus, the production staff, extra talent, set design, construction, dressing, operations, wardrobe, makeup,

---

8   Stroheim, in his Eulogy for D.W. Griffith.

lighting, rigging, cameras, grips, special effects, and sound mixers all melded with the uncanny flow and synchronicity of a production stripboard that is the core of professional cinematography. One look back through the two overgrown palm trees that tower over the gated entrance of the cemetery, and I realized that further specifications would not be necessary—for there in the background, riveted onto the otherwise desolate hardscrabble of the hillside, stood the refurbished HOLLYWOOD sign, as big and bold and determinate as any of the cinema production *de rigueur*, as ominous artistically as any of the chalk-white tombstones in my view.

What I *did* find somewhat odd was the unscripted scene in which Zilch himself was leaning into the open coffin of Byron Harmsway, for he appeared to be searching intently for something underneath the cadaver or possibly in the dead man's pockets. He waved the camera man away and continued frantically for something, rifling through the pockets and the bedding like a man possessed. It was easy to tell from his body language that the object in question was not found, and I could now surmise with some degree of confidence, but still no material confirmation, that this frenzied search had something to do with Kaltrina Dahl and the allegedly stolen object.

I didn't have to wait long for the wrap party and my scheduled postproduction appointment with Zilch, for it was an open-and-shut case of Hollywood filmmaking, punctuated, at times, by the slating of particular *shots* and *takes* marked for sound by a clapperboard, until the film and the coffin were both in the can. As rapidly as the production crew appeared out of nowhere, they likewise disappeared with all and sundry equipment into unmarked trucks and vans and nondescript vehicles that move around this town largely unnoticed on any given day. Zilch signaled for me to join him as he headed away from the remaining mourners, past the graves of John Huston and Fay Ray, to the back plots of Hollywood Forever, which are nearly abutting the walled environs of Paramount Studios.

I waited until we were out of earshot of the others before saying, "So you actually *did* see Byron Harmsway the evening before he died?"

Zilch came to a halt and spun around dramatically to face me.

"I told you that I might, and I didn't say that I hadn't," he quipped.

Behind Zilch was an array of fountains spouting away in an elongated reflecting pool—the sunken tree-lined entranceway to the raised tomb of Douglas Fairbanks, it turned out. I veered my gaze pointedly from the ornate marble memorial and looked into the blazing eyes of my client.

"You also told me that you had nothing to do with this business. Are you sure that the dearly departed Byron Harmsway didn't offend you in some way?"

"Look, Metropolis, I'd snuff out the sun if it offended me—or I'd have someone from special effects do it for me. But it's not the sun or even the lecherous man that offends me. All visible objects are but pasteboard masks to me; it is some despicable, inscrutable, unreasoning thing that puts the molding on their features. The idea of Harmsway galls me. Yes, he bothered me. But he is only a mask—it is the emptiness behind the mask I chiefly hate. And it is the emptiness behind the man that I intended to eliminate."

"You're speaking cinematically, I suppose?" I asked.

The sun, getting ready to wink out for the day, painted the trees behind him in a glorious golden color.

"If you say so."

"I mean, you don't really mean what you're saying literally, do you?"

"In Hollywood, we take our illusions seriously."

"In that case, let me ask you directly: Did you or did you not have anything to do with Byron Harmsway's death, be it murder or suicide?"

"No and yes. No, I did not murder him, and yes, I had something to do with his suicide. You see, I agreed to produce his latest novel—as I said, to throw him a bone. But he and I both knew that it was a piece of garbage, we both *understood* that it was a piece of garbage, and we both knew that neither of us would ever produce anything but garbage ever again. And what's worse, we both knew *why*."

"Can you tell me?" I asked Zilch outright.

"Why, it's all about Kaltrina, of course. He was under her influence, or should I say, the lack thereof. All I did was tighten the screw by helping him to feel *finished*."

"That's either the kindest or the cruelest thing I have ever heard."

"You might say that Kaltrina and I finished him off."

"But you don't really believe that, Mister Zilch? You can't actually believe that?"

"I'm telling you about a situation, as it exists, as it was created. Neither you nor I have to believe it. In other words, Mister Philosopher, welcome to my world."

A distinct wave of anxiety coursed through my mind, followed by an uncanny feeling of nausea. I struggled to regain my philosophical composure in the midst of an acute bout of existential malaise. How do you manage to get beyond philosophical reasoning without resorting to arguments that are again philosophical? Is this a classic Cartesian problem—to think beyond thinking? Should I attempt to regain my perspective by constructing para-logical arguments that appeal to humanistic or poetic or coercive moralistic reasonings? I decided, instead, to abstain from argument altogether. Rather, I would accept what Zilch *means* to say as something very personal and thus decidable.

"Your world seems to be perfectly suited to the self-defeating," I said. "Perhaps we are also finished here."

"Snap out of it, Metropolis. I'm going to make it up to poor, pitiful, suicidal Byron Harmsway. I'm going to give him a far better afterlife than he ever had in reality. I'm going to make it my personal responsibility to send him off with a content-rich afterlife. It will be eternal, it will be recurrent, and there will be residuals. And I need you now more than ever. I need you to follow up on a lead that I got from Harmsway before he died. Do you want me to tell you or not? Do you want me to show you or not?"

"Go on," I said with renewed assurance that this might, at the very least, be entertaining.

He reached into his jacket pocket and pulled out a photograph, cruelly folded in half, yet clearly discernable as a headshot of a glamorous Hollywood starlet in a black evening gown. She was convincingly blond. Her face was more than beautiful; it was recognizable. She had the striking profile of a well-developed female ingénue, the fresh, exciting smile of a young bride, the dramatic arrest of an emotion held to the very edge of desire, with the kind of twinkle in the eye that makes a man want to leap tall buildings.

"She looks very familiar, Mister Zilch. She looks very much like that actress who was shot in the face by that music producer. What was her name?" I asked, inquisitive.

"Darla Darkcity, and she was *allegedly* shot in the face," Zilch corrected me.

"Well, if you want to split hairs," I said, "she was definitely shot in the face. I remember those photographs all too well. The only thing *alleged* about the sordid affair was the one who pulled the trigger. It was not clear whether it was him or her."

"Right you are." Zilch smiled, thrusting the picture in my direction. "And now that your memory is working overtime, take a good look at the headshot, and don't even think about pardoning the pun."

I took the photo and studied it closely.

"It really looks like Darla Darkcity," I concluded, "but it doesn't look *exactly* like her. As I recall, Darla was somewhat older than this when she died. This is either an earlier headsh—I mean, *portrait* of Darla or it's someone else who could be her twin sister." I looked up, and my attention was drawn to the lengthening shadows that played eerily upon the marble walls of a cavernous mausoleum, a mausoleum that held the earthly remains of Rudolf Valentino and Peter Lorre, among so many others. Suddenly, a feeling of uncanniness and dread emerged with a chill of remembrance, like echoes that speak in the phrases of death and anguish: "*Has it not become colder ... Is not night continually closing in on us ... Do we hear nothing yet of the noise of the gravediggers who are burying ... Do we not smell anything yet of ... decomposition ... How shall we comfort ourselves ... Who will wipe this blood off ... What water is there for us to clean ourselves ... What festivals of atonement ... What sacred games shall we have to invent ... Is not the greatness of this deed too great for us?*"[9]

"What on earth are you mumbling about, Metropolis? If you have something to say about this, spit it out!"

"I'm sorry, Mister Zilch, but the very thought of murder makes my skin crawl. I tend to get a bit claustrophobic when I'm forced to imagine a world without a semblance of virtue or decency. Perhaps you should really hire a *private investigator* for your purposes. I may be

---

9   Nietzsche, Parable of the Madman from *The Gay Science*

too sensitive with my philosophical positivism and my hyperaesthetic perceptions to be of any more use to you in this area of investigation."

"Let me be the judge of that," said Zilch as he handed me a handkerchief to wipe the noticeable sweat from my brow. "Just spit it out, man. Tell me what's on your mind, and I'll decide if it is useful to me or not. After all, I am the paying customer, aren't I?"

"I don't know the cause exactly, but here in this graveyard of the 'classic' movie stars, I was thinking—aloud I'm afraid—about Friedrich Nietzsche when he was confronted by the greatest murder in all of history. At first, he felt like a madman, and then he fell silent in the face of all his listeners. And they too were silent in the gloom, and they all stared at him in astonishment. And then he responded quite dramatically: as he smashed his own lantern to the ground, he shouted out that he had come too early, that his time had not yet arrived, that some tremendous event was still on its way, wandering, wandering, wandering through the aeons on its way to finally reach the eyes and ears of mankind. He said that the lightening and the thunder requires time, that the light from the distant stars requires time, that some deeds require time even after they are done, before they can be seen and heard. And then he said, and I quote, '*This deed is still more distant from them than the most distant stars—and yet they have done it themselves.*'" I was now sweating profusely from head to toe.

"Tell me more!" demanded Zilch, moving in closer as he listened intently.

"I think that Nietzsche, in ascribing the guilt of the murder, was somehow referring to *us*!" I told him the unvarnished truth, as if I had just found it out for myself.

"Well now, that's a damn good story, Metropolis. It's a tad melodramatic for modern tastes, but I like it well enough. I think I'll keep you around. You never know when your philosophical madman might come in handy."

Zilch directed me to follow him back across Maple Avenue to the banks of the cemetery lake, where he situated himself on a marble bench that happened to be the grave marker of the late Tyrone Power.

"It's not actually a headshot. It's a positive print from a director's dailies," he said with an unmistakable note of chagrin.

"You mean this photograph was taken directly from the daily rushes of a movie? But it looks more like museum-quality portrait photography to me. I don't understand."

"Neither do I, Metropolis. Neither do I. But if I'm not mistaken—and in matters of cinematography, I rarely am—then there is one hell of a new director in this town."

"How does this photograph tie in with Kaltrina Dahl?" I asked. As I joined him on Tyrone's bench, I realized that we were sitting on carved letters that formed a line from Hamlet, Act V, Scene ii: *"Now cracks a noble heart. Good night, sweet prince; and flights of angels sing thee to thy rest!"*

Zero Vaynilovich looked me in the eyes with a look of abject sadness that I will never be able to forget as long as I live.

"Find this new director in town, and you'll find Kaltrina Dahl," was all he said.

5. Allure of the Casting Couch

It was clear to me that we were dealing with a serial benefactress of the most effusive and insidious nature, entering into each personal relationship with a flourish of romantic evocation that beholds the promise of endless exaltation and everlasting love, empowering the mind with awe-inspiring visions of grandeur and lovemaking with a glowing passion that instigates man's ennoblement, magnifying every beat of the heart with a blissful surge of confidence and a flaming elation that approaches the very brink creativity itself, only to watch with inexorable coldness as it all withers on the vine, only to leave in the secrecy of silence, like a proverbial thief in the night. Somehow, without even meeting this Blue Dahlia, I know it is so, for I have seen the inexorable sadness that is impervious to pleas or persuasion. I have seen the intransigent sorrow, the hunger and the thirst.

I assured Zero Vaynilovich that I would help in any way that I could, and he returned to the wrap party that was clambering in the Chandler Gardens section of the Hollywood Forever cemetery. Not personally being in a partying mood, I found myself thinking of Emerson, who once said that *"Character is always known"* and that *"Murder will speak out of stone walls,"*[10] as I walked among the monuments across the Griffith Lawn, across the Pathway of Remembrance, through the Garden of Memory, to the gift shop and tours building, which was still open for business. I inquired as to the remote possibility that one Darla Darkcity might be buried here at Hollywood Forever, and I was very nearly correct; she was not so much buried as she was permanently on display. I was directed to a large chapel complex at the northwest

---

10   Ralph Waldo Emerson's Address to the Divinity College of Cambridge.

boundary of the cemetery. The chapel itself served as an elaborate entranceway leading to a central columbarium rotunda flanked by burial colonnades. An antique hearse was parked outside under the vaulted archways.

I entered the chapel narthex with the omnipresence of death still heavy on my mind. A pair of large, impressionistic, surrealistic paintings of a personified soul walking into the light stood prominently like sentinels, one on each side of the doorway leading into the chapel nave. In both cases, there was a shadow-image, vaguely human in its proportions, entering into a sepulchral space, at once hollow and deep and painted in grave funereal tones. Yet the vaguely recognizable human figure was embraced by a billowing expanse of something that was discernibly more luminous than the somber surroundings. The painting on the left-hand side of the arched entrance was somewhat more blurry and subjective in its surrealistic rendering, while the painting on the right was more geometric with grim vault-like walls converging upon the scene. In both cases, the artistic effect was remarkably similar. A major case of claustrophobia descended eerily upon my nervous system, accompanied by a palpable, almost oppressive feeling of unbridled uncanniness.

It was as if I was somehow frozen in time, struggling to come to grips with this discernable, nearly overwhelming feeling, when I remembered that Freud himself had attempted to address what he called "*The Uncanny*," although he was quick to assure his readers that "*Only rarely does the psychoanalyst feel compelled to engage in aesthetic investigations.*"[11] Yes, indeed, it was beginning to make sense to me. The brash psychiatrist's reluctance to deal with the theatrical aesthetics of the moment was equaled only by his obvious compulsion to embrace it. What began as a would-be science of the enigma soon found itself deeply, inadvertently implicated in the elusive enigmas of the dramatic arts. Clearly, I would have to rely on my own resources from here on out.

The Uncanny I was experiencing at this threshold of forever and eternity was not as Freud had suggested, a mere childhood dread or a suppressed fear, like some fictional Sandman who might come in the night to collect the eyes of naughty boys and girls and carry them off to

---

11   Sigmund Freud's essay on *The Uncanny*.

the half moon to be pecked upon by hooked owl's beaks.[12] We adults are agreed that there is no question of intellectual uncertainty here. We moderns should be able to detect the sober truth behind the dread with the superiority of our rational minds. Yet this knowledge did not lessen the impression of the uncanniness in the least degree. Thus the theory of intellectual uncertainty is apparently incapable of explaining this ghastly feeling of *unheimlichkeit*,[13] this intense impression of dread. Moreover, when push comes to shove at the brink of the abyss, the psychiatrist simply cuts and runs: *"Before the problem of the creative artist analysis must, alas, lay down its arms"*[14] Still, *The Uncanny* in dramatic art remains.

Perhaps then, it is not the fantastic tales of yore or even the psychoanalytic association with a fear of being robbed of one's eyes, the fear of going blind, that sparks this dreadful angst. Surely, it is not the fear of being lost-in or even blinded-by the light depicted in those two large sentinel paintings that aroused this awful feeling of intense uncanniness, this inescapable feeling of dread, this unremitting anxiety that shivers my spine and now offends my widely opened eyes. Perhaps it is something else entirely.

More likely, it is the *doubling* of the personages in these paintings that triggered the acute effect—these paintings that show the same impressionistic, surrealistic phenomena in a similar but slightly different way. It is quite possible that the theme of the *"Double,"* or *"Doppelgänger,"* is at hand, whether its reflection is in mirrors, in shadows, in artistic renderings, in elusive impressions, or in association with guardian spirits ... with belief in the soul in peril ... with the primal fears and forebodings of death. It is quite possible that the theme of the *"Body Double"* is what links mankind to murder, a part of ourselves to each untimely death. That psychic foil that seeks to preserve itself against extinction, that counterpart of man construed by us all in the language of dreams that seek to provide an assurance of our immortality, that mysterious double that dominates the mind

---

12   Freud's literary critique of "The Sand-Man" in Hoffmann's *Nach-tstücken*.

13   German, Uncanniness.

14   Freud in *Dostoevsky and Parricide*.

of the child and of primitive man, brings with it *the uncanny*, our very own harbinger of death.

As a somewhat contemplative and admittedly oversensitive spectator, I had to somehow brace myself to carry forth—for the sake of professional curiosity if for nothing else. I had to force myself, literally and figuratively, to move beyond these two eerie paintings that strangely guarded the entranceway. Moreover, I had to try and see for myself just how closely this *photographic double*—now folded in my sweaty hand—how closely this fatalistic headshot resembled the actual image, the impression, the death mask of this newest Hollywood legend, forthwith and forever on display. Finally, I managed to proceed, *sotto voce,* with poetic fortitude, if not with stoic resolve.

"Columbaria to the right of me, columbaria to the left of me, columbaria in front of me, fame's ashes asunder," I charged forth with poetical impetus. "Into the jaws of Death, into the mouth of Hell," I strode, or more aptly, I blundered. Hastily, I walked past my own *mal à son aise*,[15] through the darkening *locus suspectus*,[16] with its unattenuated *unheimlichkeit*, its rows of empty pews, its conspicuously empty podium, until I got to the inner sanctum of a domed columbarium rotunda bedecked with a multitude of brass mausoleum chambers. Then I crept up the spiral staircase step-by-step to the second floor.

I found myself surrounded by a ghostly scene of yawning arches and eyeless windows arrayed in hollow tiers. The setting sun, which scarcely entered the columbary vaults, was of little comfort, illuminating the scene with a gauzy light similar to what one might find in an unattended attic or an old, abandoned mansion. The sepulchral niches were arrayed in a grim circus like so many schoolhouse lockers, only twice as wide with thick glass windows and half as high, for the ashes of the dead were layered one upon the other. A social stratification was notable in that some of the mausoleum chambers were geometrically larger than the others. Still, one had to venture close to peer into these murky windowed chambers in order to view the ornate funereal urns, the somber faded photographs, the porcelain figurines, the collections of once-treasured objects on display.

---

15   French, feelings of discomfort.

16   Latin, uncanny place.

My acute awareness of death, heightened by the overbearing silence of the tomb, made all the more impression on me, as my own reluctant footsteps echoed in the gloom. And then it came upon me again, that wretched feeling of claustrophobia, that visceral shiver I so precisely associate with the act of murder, the mere thought of murder, the very concept of murder. Only this time, the dreaded feeling did not descend upon me in a wave—it felt as if it were about to touch me on my shoulder, to grab me from behind. I wheeled around in a state of panic, and there she was. Across the tenebrous expanse of the circular room, Darla Darkcity was looking out of her window, smiling out of her window, plaiting a dark red love-knot into her long blond hair.

I crossed the room with trembling trepidation. Looking at the portrait of Darla, trying to figure out what to do next, trying to figure out why a *private eye* might not be a far better choice here than a hyperaesthetic *perspicuous eye*, trying to figure out that one move on the philosophical chessboard, that one muscular shift of assumptions, that one lordly leap of logic and/or language and/or premise and/or theme that would enable me to move in such untimely meditations beyond the mere ugliness of a will to murder, the ugliness of such a human, all too human, a motivation to move beyond the birth of this dark tragedy, beyond my personal claustrophobia that owes its provenance to the ultimate devaluation of all values—the crushing act and total annihilation of a living, breathing thing of beauty.

With only a dim apprehension of my purpose, in the funereal aloofness that was really quite chilling, I gazed back and forth between the cinematic *still* I held tightly in my hand and the life-size portrait of Darla Darkcity, still smiling at me from the grave. The perception of *the uncanny* now evolved into a full-blown case of metaphysical vertigo, with its accompanying feelings of nausea and alarming aspects of anxiety, which were never more present. Actually, I was feeling kind of seasick, but my job called out for more. I was striving to comprehend the substance of Darla's lovely smile when her face, at first just ghostly, turned a whiter shade of pale. It was then that I began to notice the sublime subtlety of living colors within this dim and dusty twilight of the idols that shown with an austere solemnity throughout the upper vaults of the funereal rotunda.

One flower stood out from all the clusters of white orchids that hung from the wall in brass vases, stood out from the bouquets of red roses on the many cards that were lined up along the edges of the glass windows, stood out from the arrangements of yellow day lilies and pink carnations that rested peacefully in sympathy vases on the floor. There, wedged in the metallic frame, just to the left of Darla's forward-leaning shoulder, slightly above the crown of the ivory urn that held her cremated ashes, wedged tightly between the frame and the glass, was a picture of a singular solitary flower—a dahlia—painted in a distinctively brilliant shade of blue.

I tried to keep my hands from shaking despite a great pounding of the heart as I carefully removed the card from its death grip and opened it like a book.

Dearest Darla,

Your Death will be avenged by the Ascension

of the Art!

With All my Love,

Manifesta

I carefully replaced the card in its Hollywood Forever frame, and I rapidly retraced my steps.

The impatient growls of the Porsche's engine turned to high-pitched screams as I whipped out of the cemetery driveway and wound out the gears down the sainted boulevard.

.   .   .

Early the next morning, I stretched my own frame like a personal establishing shot and yawned out over the vacuous smog of the Los Angeles Basin from the loft window of my humble abode in the Hollywood Hills. I showered, shaved, spritzed on some high-priced cologne, downed some home-brewed coffee, and donned my finest corporate attire, rendered business casual by the purposeful absence of a tie. Then I awakened all ten cylinders of the Porsche Carrera GT and headed into town, hoping to make some headway on this case, realizing full well that Zilch wanted me to follow up personally on this curious photographic lead rather than have his less-than-perspicuous goons gumshoeing all over the place, gumming up the works.

It wouldn't be easy. I knew that much. I couldn't just go to Central Casting in Burbank and ask point-blank for the official list of celebrity photo-doubles, stand-ins, and look-alikes that might lead me to the *auteur* of the remarkable *mise-en-scène*. No, it wasn't going to be that easy—not in this town.

Hollywood is and always has been a closed shop, enticing and alluring in its open invitation to voyeuristic appeal; yet it can be exasperating, if not infuriating, with its practiced and nearly perfected standoffishness, not to mention its operational and financial machinations that are entirely inscrutable to outsiders. The simple fact of the matter is that Hollywood is a union town and has been since the 1930s. Every actor, writer, director, camera operator, stagehand, sound technician, pyrotehnician, editor, assistant editor, special effects person, scenic artist, graphic artist, animator, and cartoonist has a technical guild and/or craft union to call their very own and vice versa—not to mention the projectionists. I knew this to be true ever since I wrote that chapter on the *Subjugation of the Angelic*, which was included in **Lost Angels Pantheon** against the better judgment of my publisher. And I was counting on this underlying bulwark of solidarity to help me complete my next move.

I was heading directly to the headquarters of the Screen Actors Guild on Wilshire, counting on the inviolability of "Global Rule One" to serve as a springboard for my strategic move in the desired, but as yet to be determined, direction. Global Rule One, as it is stamped on the back of each and every screen actor's membership card, states that "*No member shall work as a performer for any producer who has not executed a basic minimum agreement with the Guild which is in full force and effect.*" It is this axiomatic forbidding that I planned to use to my advantage.

Inside the Screen Actors Guild, I encountered a scene straight out of Dostoyevsky's *Notes from the Underground*. There was a sick man, a spiteful man, and an unattractive woman. One might suspect that their collective livers were diseased—and that they weren't going to be getting better anytime soon. Much like a retinue one might expect from an antiquated government service, I was shuttled from the offices of one sick or spiteful official to the next—each one more rude than the last, each one apparently taking pleasure in being so. In the course of my progress, I was made to feel like an unwelcome petitioner, while the succession of spiteful officials ground their teeth, each betraying a glimmer of intense joy with the dramatic prospects of making someone else miserable. (A poor jest, I know, but I will not scratch it out.)

I played along with the bureaucratic psychodrama, of course; after all, I *was* a petitioner, though I was feigning to be a timid one. That is, until I encountered a particularly uppity individual that I could not endure, one that simply would not be civil, and who clanked his gilded authority in a disgusting way. When I politely informed him that I was inquiring into the whereabouts of an actress that may or may not be involved in a production that may or may not be legitimately sanctioned by the Screen Actors Guild, he responded violently, as if he was used to scaring sparrows at random and amusing himself by it.

"If you aren't one of us, we will shut you down!" he shouted at me in a moment of the acutest spleen. "Our message to your damned Indie production is this: If you aren't one of us, we won't allow you to make movies! If you don't let us paint your wagon, we won't let you roll with it!"

"But, sir," I protested, "I didn't say that I have anything to do with an independent production company operating outside of the SAG–Indie guidelines. I am simply inquiring as to the actual identity and credentials of an actress who may or may not be operating in compliance with Global Rule One."

"Well now. If you aren't *production* or *talent*, who the hell are you?"

"I'm not at liberty to say. But I have certain information that relates directly to your so-called talent, and I need certain information in exchange."

My refusal to be intimidated seemed to sicken the ill-mannered individual all the more, tormenting him to the point of convulsions that craved an outlet.

"This had better be for real. I'm warning you," he threatened as he punched the buttons on the intercom and transferred me to the next level of organizational bureaucracy. I happened to notice, while I was leaving his office, that the preeminently limited creature was shaking his head, mumbling to himself, "*We will drive you out … spend you out … wait you out …*" as if he were practicing for the next collective host of sparrows.

I could tell that I had arrived at the vertex of my journey into the labyrinth of the Screen Actors Guild by the plaque that read "Scab Finders Group" outside the door. Once inside the stately office, my perspicacity was immediately offended by three horrifying sights. First and foremost was the leering face of an otherwise perfectly proportioned woman, a face that appeared to have been carved up and reassembled by a bevy of inept plastic surgeons in accordance with some freakish ideal of feminine youth and beauty that might be considered curious or interesting in the radical context of a cubist painting, but here, the foremost countenance of a statuesque middle-aged woman, could only be considered tragic. The second horrifying sight was the number of official-looking diplomas, degrees, certificates, and licenses that hung on the paneled wall behind the desk, framed admissions that attested to the fact I was facing an attorney at law. The third and no-less horrifying sight was the number of headshots that covered the flanking walls—headshots of actors and actresses pilfered, presumably, by union moles from casting sessions of suspected scabs, headshots from nonunion movies, shows, and/or commercials, headshots that identified the unfortunate dramatist as a nonbeliever, someone to be fingered, someone to be made an example of, someone whose career in the movies would come to an end before it had even begun.

"Do come in, Doctor Metropolis," she said. Nothing moved but her corpulent lips. I felt the stares of the doomed and dying starlings that would never see the lamplight.

"Nice gallery you have here," I said. "Are they all *Wanted Dead or Alive*, or do they simply fade to black?"

"Any artist who works for an independent filmmaker who won't sign with us will be denied SAG membership for an unspecified period of time. And without SAG membership, they will never be allowed to work for a major studio. So in effect, you have answered your own question—they simply fade to black."

"So that's how it is? If you don't pay us money, join our gang, and do what we say, we will prevent you from ever working in this town again. It sounds to me like a policy of blacklisting, which appears rather paradoxical from the perspective of Hollywood history, don't you think?"

"I'm not paid to think or to examine the ironies of history and philosophy as you are, Doctor Metropolis. And by the way, you're currently on our list ... or didn't you know that?"

"No, I didn't."

"Well, you are. But you're still welcome to sit here with me," she said, motioning to a large davenport, "while I try to convince you to change your wicked ways." She and her unnerving *moue* rose from the executive desk chair, slowly, deftly crossing the room on black stiletto heels, slowly, seductively closing and locking the outer office door, and then seating herself immediately beside me with her right hand placed firmly on my knee.

"I'm a great admirer of yours, Joe. May I call you Joe? It's not often that I get to converse with a man of your prominence." As she spoke, her hand moved up my thigh. "The men around here are so small-minded—so full of pomp without circumstance—I long to meet a man of your caliber, a man of your towering intellect."

I placed my own hand onto hers to slow, if not to abate, her advances.

"I need your help in identifying an actress and her employer that may be of mutual interest to us." I reached into my jacket for the folded photograph, and as I did, her hand began to roam. I tried to distract her with the headshot and a modicum of the backstory, but it wasn't going to work.

"Yes, Joe. I can be a big help to you, that is, if I want to. I have a photographic memory and a great knack for faces." Her hand was now moving over my lap. "Let me hold it, Joe. Let me see it. Let me have it, please."

I handed her the photograph, which momentarily halted her manual explorations, but only momentarily. I could sense the crowd of faces watching us from across the room, staring out at my predicament from their frameless perches like an attentive audience looking on. I could feel the unseen faces on the wall behind me. How many of them had been in this very same position? How many others had sat on this same *casting couch*? I could detect that common theme of underlying desire on their faces: that desire to be discovered, that look of longing that stares past all the uncomfortable realities of life and entreats, and entreats.

"Well? Can you help me or not? I don't have all day. I have places to go, things to do, people to talk to ..." I was being offish and brusque, I know, but I was undecided and somewhat put off by all appearances.

"Don't be that way, Joe. Don't be unkind. I can help you find your actress and her outlaw director, but you have to ask me nicely. Can you ask me nicely, Joe?"

"I'm sorry if I seem to be impatient. I don't mean to be rude, and I do appreciate your personal interest in my case. I'm flattered by your attention, but—"

"Then be flattered, Joe. Just be flattered. I am, shall I say, a fervent admirer. Let me admire you in my own way." The lady lawyer began to unbutton my shirt. I stopped her at my belt by lifting her head with my fingers beneath her carved chin. Her breasts heaved with anticipation; her face shined with wantonness. "Let me hold you, Joe. I want to feel the strength of a man I truly admire."

That face—I almost winced—that ghoulish deformed face. It was a shipwrecked face, wrecked beyond any denial, ruined beyond any overlooking. Somehow, I stilled my immediate reactions and summoned my professional perspicacity. I looked deep into the eyes of the woman, and I smiled, for there, beyond the ravages of the inept surgeries, beyond the scars and deformity of time, beyond the ordinary, the unattractive, the unremarkable, was the desire to be beautiful, that ageless, timeless yearning to be loved.

Overcome by compassion and the reluctant thrill of all those who had lain on this very couch before me, I entered into the Theater of the Amative, the realm of make-believe.

"I am truly flattered," I said as I unbuckled my own belt.

It was then that I began to hear the music of Tchaikovsky's *Swan Lake*. It was then that I began to feel the gripping pull of the drama, the sadness, the pathos, the tragedy of the Black Swan, that merely mortal woman who could not measure up to the inflated imaginings of the young Prince, that Woman-of-the-Palace who could not compete with the idealized Dream of Beauty that exists only in the imagination, only at Swan Lake, only in the dark. The pitiable Black Swan is rejected out of hand, and for what? For being a veritable *fashionista*, for striving with all her feminine wiles and intelligence to become the object of the Prince's desire, for striving to make herself conform to his ideals of beauty and become his mate for life?

I did not resist when the lawyer lady broached the subject again with her refined feminine delectations, advocating her cause with such perfervid pulses of assertiveness. My resolve had stiffened considerably but had not yet reached the point of contention, for she was on a roll and could not be interrupted. So I allowed her to indulge herself fully in this one aspect of impassioned oratory, at least for the moment.

I saw, or rather, I felt, the faces on the walls looking at me again, some of them with warning, with disapproval, with desire, yes, but desire that was tinctured with alarm.

I lifted her head again, this time with both hands, and I heard myself saying, "I'm not sure I can allow this to continue. I'm beginning to feel somewhat used—somewhat objectified!"

"You can stop me any time you want, Joe. But then you won't get what you want." Her breathing slowed, and her demeanor became more formal. "I can give you what you want, Joe. I definitely have what you want. I know exactly what you want. But you won't get it without my help." She grinned, knowing that she was unduly convincing.

She resumed her insinuations with renewed vigor, drawing upon my stamina, overcoming my resistance, reveling in my predicament, lashing out and thrashing upon the principle of the thing until I could neither resist nor hold out any longer. I was swooning in my resolve to keep myself unto myself, torn between the modest impulse to extricate myself from the situation and my mounting urge to delve more deeply into this conundrum of the casting couch. Just when I was reaching a definitive point of explication, she suddenly stopped, leaned back, unbuttoned her white silk blouse, and unclipped her black brassiere revealing nothing less than perfection of form and function. It was then that I noticed that this particular davenport was, in actuality, a convertible sofa, converting effortlessly from sofa to bed.

When I say that she was statuesque, I am not exaggerating in the least. Her perfectly tanned body was a sculpture in and of itself, shaped and toned and polished to an adamantine gleam. Below the neck, she was dazzling; she was astonishing; she was breathtaking. Here in the Theater of the Amative, she was showing, she was disclosing, she was alluring, she was becoming, and she was waiting for me to make my move.

There is magic in the theater, magic that is often missed in the whole of the plastic arts. Magic that is known to occur only rarely in the movies, or even in books, try as they might to capture it, try as they might to recreate it. It is the natural gift of selective perception, an adaptive birthright of all human kind, that is, the ability to see only that which is desirable and pleasurable, to see only that which is in keeping with our illusions of a reality that we constantly construct. Suddenly, there was such a magical moment on the davenport that I can scarcely describe.

This marble statue of a woman spoke to me from across the vast chasm of incredulity. "I want to be one of your angels, Joe. Make me one of your angels."

The ghoulish and horrific features and the shipwrecked face had all but disappeared in the light of this luminous, amorous appeal. Vanished also were the arms that needed either twisting or restraint. I found myself gazing at a living, breathing statue of the *Venus of Cyrene*, regaled in all her naturalistic splendor, adorned with a confidence of overwhelming gracefulness, portrayed with all her headless femininity, naked, alluring, magnificent, and tangible to the touch. Of course, I realized full well that this precious statue-in-my-mind was merely a facsimile, a replica of a Greek statue, a reproduction of a Greek ideal, which, in reality, is never to be found. Nevertheless, I convened my powers of creative imagination and embraced the Goddess of Love.

6. Psycho Killer, Qu'est-ce Que C'est?

The darkness of the evening came on like a double shot of tequila, but I was feeling pretty good—too good to notice the incipient danger that was lurking around every corner, too good to mind the mucilaginous grime that permeated the very sidewalks of West Hollywood. I was walking north on Havenhurst, where I had parked my wheels-of-the-week to avoid announcing my arrival at the most notorious château this side of perdition. Crossing Sunset in a jay-walking hurry, I sauntered up to the turreted castle that was perched ever so secretively on a hill high above the Strip. I had made dinner reservations under an assumed name, which got me past the host of wary attendants and gained me admittance into the 1920s-era, Prague-like ambience of the Château Marmont.

In addition to the inscription of this particular address, I had a ten-digit number in my pocket, and I wasn't afraid to use it to my client's advantage. I whipped out my cell phone and nonchalantly thumbed the numbers with the irrational confidence of a kleptomaniac.

"My name is Joe. I know all about you and Manifesta. I'm downstairs in the lobby, waiting for you to join me for dinner. I'm tired and hungry, and I don't like to be kept waiting."

Amazingly, it worked. I didn't have to wait for long.

She wore a brownish speckled tweed skirt, a tailored blouse, and a golden choker necklace. Her stockings were as sheer as the five sensual pleasures of desire, and she was showing a lot of leg. Her eyes were hidden behind brown oversized sunglasses, and her blond hair was tastefully cloistered under the auspices of a big floppy hat. She moved slowly, as though there was pressure and tension in the air.

"Good evening, Scarlett. So nice of you to join me," I said without a hint of solicitude.

"You've got a lot of nerve coming here to threaten me. What are you, some kind of blackmailer?" Behind the nonchalance in her tone, I sensed a slight suggestion of curiosity. "All I can say, mister, is you've got a lot of nerve."

"I've also got a lot of backstory on you, Scarlett, which gives me, shall we say, a certain amount of verisimilitude. Now, if you'll behave yourself and avoid making a cliché out of this scene, I'll treat you to a nice dinner, and I'll explain to you my purpose and my nonthreatening agenda. That is, unless you would prefer me to be threatening."

"No, I would not!" she said as she leaned forward seductively, adjusting the angle of her hat with both of her hands. "I just want you to know that I'm good at keeping secrets—I mean, when I have to, I mean, when I want to."

"I know exactly what you mean, Scarlett," I said as I placed my arm around her waist and escorted her into the dining room. "I know exactly what you mean. Still, I intend to convince you that the dramatic revelation of secrets from the backstory is a very useful theme in narratology. It's recommended as far back as Aristotle's *Poetics*."

"Really? I didn't know that," said Scarlett, warming to my embrace.

"Really," I affirmed as I adjusted my hand more firmly around her waist and directed her to our reserved table. Apparently, my sojourn into the heady realm of the *Venus of Cyrene* had improved both my outlook and my moves.

The dining room was intimate, like a Viennese coffeehouse, and eternally chic, with brocade-covered walls, wavy-edged mirrors, and an antique chandelier. The resident clientele had that look-at-me/don't-look-at-me ambivalence that is common to this *sui generis* locale. I told Scarlett that I was tipped off by an associate at the Screen Actors Guild, but I wanted to avoid overplaying my hand. I said that I only wanted information from her, in the service of a client, and that she herself was not the target. Scarlett began to relax with the arrival of the champagne-tossed arugula, shrimp, and blood orange salad. By the time we got to the meatless lasagna, with eggplant, roasted tomatoes, and herbed parmesan crust, we were chatting away like old friends.

She told me that she was staying at the Château with the rest of a determinate cast until some kind of West Hollywood screening was over. It was all very hush-hush—which, in reality, meant that she was just dying to tell someone. They were all supposed to meet on Friday night at the corner of Sunset and Londonderry to witness some kind of cinematic happening, and then they were to meet again for the screening of their own underground film. From what I could gather, this Manifesta was one great producer–director, some kind of mad genius, some kind of *Auteur Extraordinaire*—a true mastermind: incredibly wealthy, incredibly talented, driven by dark passions and a personal vision that goes way beyond the beyond. But then again, this town has seen this all before.

When she had revealed these secreted things to me, she removed the floppy hat, which previously hid everything but her charms, and then her sunglasses, which revealed the remainder of her beautiful face. It was then that the very breath in me ceased to move either in or out. The very blood in my veins turned cold at the sight of *Darla Darkcity*, as if she had reached out from her mausoleum chamber and grabbed me by the throat.

How in the world could someone have ended the life of such a beautiful, such an innately glamorous creature? What vile malevolence could be responsible? What *"imp of the perverse,"* dredged from the nethermost depths of Poe's catacombs, has been unleashed upon us? And if, indeed, this was Darla reincarnate, how could this be? I was struggling to come to grips with my own personal repugnance for the savage act of murder, my own metaphysical vertigo that comes upon me when my sense of all that is decent and orderly and intelligible is washed away in a violent flood of chaotic misanthropy that topples the temples of all that is good and leaves me in a swirling vortex of darkness with nothing to hold on to but the vivid memories and the corpse, when I heard the voice of Scarlett calling out to me in the distance.

"Doctor Metropolis? Hello, Doctor Metropolis, this is your dinner guest speaking. Earth to Doctor Metropolis!"

"I'm sorry, Scarlett. You look so much like Darla Darkcity that I think you short-circuited my brain. How in the world did they do this? This goes way beyond makeup."

"Yes, Doctor Metropolis, this goes way beyond makeup. But this is also the kind of realism that Manifesta demands of her actors and actresses."

"You called me Doctor Metropolis. You know who I really am."

"You can't hide who you are any more than I can hide from my new theatrical identity."

"And I thought I was being clever."

"You are clever, Doctor Metropolis. And you understand actors. That's how come we all know who you are. You don't think we only read screenplays, do you?"

"No, I guess not, but I did enjoy playing the tough-guy detective with you."

"So did I, Doctor Metropolis. I think I enjoyed it almost as much as you did."

"You're just being kind. But I admit I was having fun. Even before I knew exactly what, or rather, whom, you look like. And now I'm embarrassed by my own pretense."

"Don't be. If you want to know the truth, it's what we actors do. Watch carefully now," she said as she conjured the air with her hands. "Concentrate on the moment … focus on the emotion … watch for it now … wait for it …" Then she placed her hands flat on the table, leaned forward, and stared at me with a smile I could feel in both my hip pockets. "We pretend," she announced, and we began to laugh together like children.

By the time we got to dessert—it was butterscotch "silk" and coconut sorbet—I was hoping I could forget that I was a man on a mission. *Ethica* can be such a cruel mistress.

"Thank you for a lovely evening, Scarlett. I really can't remember having so much fun. And don't worry; all your secrets are safe with me."

"But it doesn't have to end so soon. You know I have my own room."

"I relish the thought, pretty lady. I truly relish the thought. However, it's too soon for me; honestly, it is. And I really came here on business. But the next time I call you up, you can be sure it's because of that smile of yours—that smile behind the mask, that smile that I can still feel in my hip pockets."

"Fair enough, you dear, sweet man. But before you go, could you do something for me? Could you tell me what kind of angel I might be?"

"Hmmm, let me think." I paused dramatically to cherish the moment. "I think that you might be ... that you might quite possibly be ... or at least you are well on your way to becoming ... a Fourth-Order Simulacrum."

"That sounds intriguing, Doctor Metropolis. But what does it mean?"

"I'm not sure we have the time—" I began to say, somewhat pretentiously.

"I'll make time, Doctor Metropolis. No one is in a hurry in this magic castle, as you can see."

She was right; there were no frenetic waiters hovering around the tables. In fact, there was a remarkable paucity of anyone actually paying attention to anyone else. It was as if some silent codes of secrecy and decorum were being enforced. The food had been ordered and served with a certain degree of efficiency, yet the staff appeared and disappeared without so much as notice being taken, with a solemn formality akin to that of protecting privacy, or perhaps it was in reverence for the dead.

"I want you to tell me what kind of angel I might be, or becoming, or whatever. And please, Doctor Metropolis, I want you to explain it to me in plain English." There was that smile again, that smile that ran straight down my spine, reached under the table, emptied out my pants pockets, and dropped my professional pretenses around my ankles.

"Very well, Scarlett, since you put it that way. A Fourth-Order Simulacrum is a postmodern extension of a philosophical tradition that goes as far back as Greek statuary, as far back as Plato's cave. You see, in his dialogue on the *Sophist*, or prince of *esprits-faux*, Plato speaks of two kinds of image making. The first is a faithful reproduction, attempting to precisely copy or duplicate the original form. The second is intentionally distorted in proportion or scale to give the viewers an *appearance* of reality, such as the distorted perspectives seen in larger-than-life statues and in monumental architecture. These constructs appear to be correct, unless they are viewed from a critical perspective, which reveals the artifice and the distortions of the truth, as it were. In this manner, Plato uses the visual arts as a metaphor for the philosophical arts and the tendency of some of the philosophers of his time to distort the truth in such a manner that it appears on the surface to be accurate, but in reality, it is considerably malformed."

"So you think of me as malformed?" she asked, as her smile disappeared behind darkening clouds.

"On the contrary, I find you incredibly attractive, incredibly lifelike, and incredibly provocative in every way. And that's what I'm getting at, if you would allow me and if you could manage to bring back that beautiful smile of yours."

My pretenses remained down about my ankles.

"The concept of the simulacrum is seen again in Nietzsche's *Twilight of the Idols*, where he argues that most modern philosophers still tend to ignore the reliable input and validity of their senses, resorting instead to dubious constructs of language and reason and ending up with a hopelessly distorted copy of reality. It's really one of our major issues in modern philosophy, Scarlett."

"Can we move on to my angel, Doctor Metropolis—the angel that I am becoming?"

"Of course we can," I said, fumbling for a shred of dignity. "You, my dear, are a Fourth-Order Simulacrum, a construct of our exceedingly postmodern times. You are not just a copy of the real; you are fast becoming a new reality, a truth in your own light. You are not just a reflection or embodiment of a historic reality; you are an Angel of the Hyperreal, and a beauteous angel at that."

"Oh, Doctor Metropolis," she breathed, her face flushed with feminine appreciation. "Tell me more." Indubitably, she had exposed that tender spot of female vulnerability and had guided me seductively to its cusp. "Tell me more," she repeated with a convivial look of encouragement. "You can't stop there," she said as her hand covered my hand. "I want you to tell me more. I want to embrace and absorb your deepest thoughts."

It wasn't easy, with Scarlett's conspicuous physiognomy, her classical psychology, and her impassioned desire displayed so vividly before me.

But somehow, I managed, and I continued to buffet and to broach the delicate subject with professional dexterity.

"Well, of the four distinctive orders of simulacrum, as in likeness or similarity, we have covered two: one, the basic reflection of reality, and two, the perversion of reality. According to the modern French theorist, Jean Baudrillard, there is a third—the pretense of reality. Well, as we discussed earlier, you actors, or should I say actresses, know all about that. And we could stop there, with *The Simple Art of Pretense*, were it not for your vastly superior potentiality. Do you want me to stop there?"

"No! No! Don't stop there. Keep going. I find your thoughts strangely exciting. Your spontaneous prose is so different from the conventional scripts we actresses are inundated with. Please, continue. You do so please me as you speak." Scarlett's head rolled gracefully back in an obvious display of overly dramatized intoxication.

"The purpose of my meandering commentary is to prepare the philosophical setting for you and the mood, in modern terms, while the real upshot of my discourse is to introduce you to the naked potentiality of the Fourth-Order Simulacrum."

"Yes," she said with her eyes closed in anticipation. "Kindly, introduce me."

"Frankly, Scarlett, you're not real; you're hyperreal. The Fourth-Order Simulacrum creates a hyperreality, or 'reality by proxy,' which bears no relation to reality whatsoever. It creates an entirely new reality, with its own premises, its own rules, its own value systems, and its own rewards. It is a satellite orbiting around an empty center. It is no more real than the Main Street attraction or the railroad station at Disneyland; it is no more real than *Westworld* or *Jurassic Park*; it has no more intrinsic value than a Federal Reserve note. According to Baudrillard, the creation of such imaginary social worlds, or hyperrealities, influences people to the extent that they collectively make believe that the artificial surroundings are real, and they may even begin to act aggressively to uphold their valued illusions. It is quite possible that the entire greater Los Angeles Basin is not real at all, but hyperreal."

As I spoke, Scarlett seemed to become tense, as if I was somehow hurting her, or about to. Ever conscious of my emotional impact on such exquisite sensibilities, I adjusted my approach to address the delicacy of the issues at hand, proceeding in a more tangential yet equally determined manner.

"But I want to assure you, my dear, that the Fourth-Order Simulacrum plays a very important role in our wayward postmodern world. Further, it is not your function as a mere body double, not the inability of our modern society to distinguish authentic reality from a contrived fantasy world, or even the perils, versus the recreational values of the imaginary arts, vapid consumerism, and illusory entertainment. I believe that you are involved in an epic drama that only you, and people attuned to what you represent, are capable of arousing."

"Yes, that's it," she said, suddenly wide-eyed and attuned to my message with rising climactic urgency. "Yes. That's it exactly. Go on. Don't you dare stop now!"

"In contrast to Friedrich Nietzsche and Jean Baudrillard, who viewed all simulacra in a negative light, I tend to agree with Gilles Deleuze, who thoroughly examines and ultimately treasures the often avenging Angel of the Hyperreal. For it is in appreciating her overarching **BEAUTY** and in grasping the sublime potentiality of her social function that we find an avenue by which dubious yet *accepted ideals* and so-called *privileged positions* of social strata can be challenged and overturned. In some situations, it is the very fondness for, the very striving for, that overarching **IDEA of BEAUTY** that can be redeeming."

Scarlett shuddered with the rising puissance of the thoughts, and then she warmed to the gratifying solace of the aesthetics.

"Now that's my kind of Philosopher," she said finally, beaming with a self-satisfied smile. "Is there any more where that came from?"

"You find a way to introduce me to this mysterious Manifesta character on Friday night, and I'll see what I can do."

. . .

Friday night in West Hollywood is a sight to behold. Everyone in motion, seriously, maniacally cruising the avenues and boulevards, bent on arriving somewhere important, all in search of something called entertainment—an agreeable occupation of the mind that evolved for hunting and gathering and learning to survive in a hostile and savage world but which now seeks out pleasure and amusement and diversion from anything and everything of the sort. People traveling hither and yon, searching for no one in particular, standing in lines waiting nonchalantly to be admitted to that state of mind called arrival.

It was going on nine o'clock when I motored past Carneys, the little yellow train going nowhere, past the long lines of consumers in attendance outside the House of Blues and the Comedy Store. I pulled the Porsche Carrera GT neatly into the parking lot at Mel's Drive-In, where I gave the valet parking attendant a fifty to stash it someplace safe for a few hours. By the time I stepped out onto the sidewalks of the Sunset Strip, there was a large crowd gathering outside the Club Monaco for no apparent reason, but the eldritch sensation of weirdness and anticipation that was spreading through the gratuitous congregation was contagious. There was an urgent feeling of something about to happen in the air that can best be described as electrical.

I was positioning myself in the midst, like a lemming, trying to gain an acceptable point of view, if not escape, when a groundswell of raised voices swept through the growing crowd and all eyes turned upward to the distant roofline of a ten-story office building across the street. The crowd began to move westward along the sidewalks and out into the street to gain a better view of side of the building, and I was swept along with the crush. Suddenly, giant sheets of gossamer fabric began to unfurl like a giant sail, illuminated by several batteries of spotlights, billowing down from the obscured environs of the rooftop along the entire length of the exterior wall, covering the high-fashion billboard advertisement that had previously adorned the side of the building. Then the spotlights suddenly went dark.

I was beginning to feel somewhat alone in the madding crowd, with all its ignoble strife, when a human hand, soft and warm, claimed mine in the darkness of the civic amphitheatre. It was Scarlett who whispered "Hello, handsome" in my ear. Even without looking, I could still sense her unforgettable smile, along with the beautiful theatrical likeness hidden behind oversized sunglasses and the brim of that big floppy hat. That, and the lovely scent of the perfume she was wearing was all a man should ever need as he stands somewhere in the darkness, waiting for the show to go on.

Another wave of raised voices accompanied the emergence of great plumes of smoke as it rose from the seams of an alleyway in the foreground, an alleyway that was completely blocked off by the tailgate of one of those nondescript production trucks. Captivated by the growing spectacle, the crowd moved further out into the congested boulevard, which soon became engrossed in gridlock as car after car stopped in its tracks and the awe-struck passengers eagerly joined in the mass confusion of the throng.

Scarlett turned and threw her arms around me to avoid being swept away with the milling chorus of Los Angelenos. A moment passed that I can scarcely describe. Her transformative face turned upward to mine ... our lips all but pressed together in longing desiderium, our bodies no longer separate but unanimous. It was only a moment, and it passed so quickly. I'm surprised I even remember it. But then I turned her around to face the steaming side of the building, holding her close with my hands on her hips. Each and every spectator now anxiously anticipated the onset of the *Aurora Theatricalis*.

It began with laser lights beaming from here and there, intersecting with perfection to produce an amazing array of dazzling numbers, counting down in midair. The audience responded to the "wow factor" by counting down in unison. But that was only the beginning. Upon reaching zero, a shimmering iconic manifestation of the name "MANIFESTA" emerged with a piercing, earsplitting sound that sparkled with such clarity in the high-frequency range that neck hairs bristled, and it loomed with such thunderous resonance in the bass notes as to vibrate the chest cavities of everyone within a three-block radius. What followed next, I can only describe as a form of Holographic Imagery, although I have never seen anything quite like it in terms of realism in either scientific or cinematic demonstrations. This was nothing like the crude 3D experience that comes and goes in theaters from time to time. This was an entirely new technology taken to a new level of artistry. It was as if we were all watching the brilliant birth of a new star.

The open-air movie began with a confrontation between two men, joined shortly by a woman whose frantic shrieks filled the empty spaces with screams of desperation. Each of the figures was immediately recognizable—immediately, vividly, unmistakably recognizable as the real live characters of a double murder mystery that had played out not so long ago on the back steps of a Westside condominium, played out nightly in the evening news, played out interminably in the courtroom dramas for months at a time. Only this time, the drama was real, all too real. The cinematography was vivid, all too vivid. And the characters were human, all too human, with the singular exception that they were many times larger than life. The combination of smoke and lasers and surround sound and intense holographic imagery created a disembodied actuality that was as astonishing as it was mesmerizing.

This was Tech Noir at its very best. And by this, I don't mean another B-movie about technophobia or some speculative strain of science fiction. Here was high technology that was not "black" but luminous, an entirely new medium that was not reflecting a fear of technology, but was utilizing advanced technology to restore the rapt authenticity of direct experience to the viewer, an experience that has been all but lost in the postmodern world. It was clearly *Noir*: by the nature of the stagecraft, the connotations of moral ambiguity, and a worldview that does not reconcile, but simply renders the absolutes of "good" and "evil." Indeed, there was bitterness, as in the bitterness of life and hope defeated, but the fear that was being created was not the fear of the high technology but the fear of what dark forces lie simmering within ourselves.

The knife swipes the air, and the audience gasps. The unarmed man takes a defensive stance, and everyone on the boulevard tenses up. The hapless woman cries out, attempting to distract and abate the vicious attacker, alas to no avail. Young women in the audience scream out, and young men clamor in protest, but the vociferous pleas from the crowd cannot prevent the slashing, which now begins in earnest, followed by a horrific repetition of point-blank stabbings. Astoundingly, the woman's head is nearly severed from her body as the violence, like hatred, is directed toward its mark. Sickened to their very souls, people begin swooning as blood and tears are falling faintly through the universe and faintly falling, like the descent of the last curtain of the last picture show, upon all the living and the dead.

And then the snuff movie was over. The civic amphitheatre was once again bathed in the blinking, flashing semidarkness of the city street on a Friday night. The crowd disbursed in every direction, and cars began to cruise again upon the Strip as if nothing had happened, but something had happened, and there was not a sentient being in attendance who could ever deny that it had.

"What do you think of my boss now?" asked Scarlett as we strolled together along the sidewalks of the hallowed boulevard.

"I am more anxious than ever to meet him, or rather, her."

"Well, tonight's your lucky night, big boy. Are you sure you're up for it?"

"You bet I am," I said, gently squeezing her hand.

"I have to warn you, though. She's not like anyone you've ever met before."

"Thanks for the warning, sweetheart. From what we've both witnessed tonight, I wouldn't expect her to be like anyone else on the planet."

"In that case, you'll find her at Ketchup, which is right down the street."

For some reason, Scarlett felt good on my arm that night. It was a good feeling to have her warm and close to me, even though she was theatrically veiled and in disguise. It was a feeling I didn't want to ruin by trying to get to the bottom of it.

Ketchup is an über-trendy joint located on the second story of a storefront known as the Sunset Millennium Complex, all decked out in white leather with red neon trimmings. We were met by a hostess and a bodyguard who was obviously screening the dinner guests this evening. Scarlett must have had the right password, for we were soon headed up the elevator and into the strange tomato-based plushness of the lounge that looks out over Sunset Boulevard through great glass windows. There was ketchup everywhere you looked: framed pictures of ketchup bottles on the walls, paintings of ketchup itself splattered on the glass doors, on the shirts of the waiters, the napkins, and even the menus. It occurred to me that the choice of restaurant was definitely not an accident, considering the subject matter of the evening.

"You're on your own, handsome," said Scarlett softly in my ear. "I'm not invited. You'll have to tell me all about it later," she said as she slipped into a white leather chair at the bar.

The hostess and the bodyguard escorted me past a line of booths filled with nouveau cinema society and LA hipsters who were deep in conversation. I noticed that there was a juicy tomato in a glass box on each of the tables, in place of flowers or candles. I was escorted to an area that was cordoned off from the main restaurant. There, I saw a stunning woman wearing a monocle and sitting alone.

She was wearing a low-cut sleeveless, backless evening gown that left little if any of the exquisite feminine contours of her upper torso to the imagination. The color of the scant but glistening fabric was, of course, Ketchup-red. Her hair was black and shining with graceful waves of sensual tresses that barely touched her shoulders. There was a weave of bright red ribbons that seemed to flow through the enchanting sea of curls. Her face, delicate and narrow of shape, with dramatic eyebrows, high cheekbones, and naturally succulent lips, was a face that could stop rush hour traffic on Interstate 405 and probably had on occasion. Her radiant beauty was, in a word, painful. For it was the kind of beauty that simply beckons to be admired—longingly and utterly admired—were it not for the painful realization that this luminous being was looking straight at you, and probably right through you, with a blazing preternaturally opened eye.

"I had no idea," was all the brilliant conversation I could muster.

"You were expecting Ayn Rand perhaps?"

"Well, yes, I mean, no, I mean, I don't know exactly what I mean."

"Well, that's a start. A shred of honesty goes a long way with me," she said as she gestured for me to be seated with an elegant wave of her cigarette holder.

As I situated myself in the spotless white leather upholstery of the oversized booth, I noticed that the cigarette holder was empty. Still, she placed it casually between her painted lips and continued to scrutinize me with her piercing monocled eye.

"Now that you mention it, there is a strong similarity between you and her, between your eyes and hers, as I remember them. That is, Ayn Rand, I mean."

"Yes?" she said, expecting me to continue.

"If you'll forgive me, her eyes had that same unrelenting intensity as yours, that same unnerving quality—at least, *I* find it unnerving. It's as if a penetrating intelligence were being communicated, in addition to a disarming sternness that serves as a warning against frivolousness."

"Well, well, Doctor Metropolis, perhaps you deserve your reputation after all. Actually, I'm flattered. For Ayn Rand was indeed a beautiful woman, a true champion of human dignity, and an intellectual of the first degree. I like to think that my work in the cinematic arts is an extension of her objectivist philosophy, an extension of her code of morality into the visual arts."

"How so?" I asked politely, for I was also a great admirer of the late Ayn Rand.

"As you know, Ayn based her entire philosophy on objective reality, on the concept that reality exists as an objective absolute, that man's mind—his reason—is his means of perceiving it, and she asserted that man needs a rational morality to sustain life. Ayn championed a new code of vigilant morality that was not based on an arbitrary faith, was not based on arbitrary whims, was not based on emotions or chauvinistic edicts, but was based on the dignity of human life as a new standard of morality.

"Furthermore," she breathed, meticulously adjusting the precise length of the telescoping cigarette holder without dropping her piercing gaze, "Ayn deplored the collective use of force and coercion and decreed entitlements that devalue human dignity. I like to think that I am, with my own advances in cinematic realism, extending her philosophical banners into the realm of a more modern feminism. By extending my cameras and computers into the darkest corners of such male-dominated abominations, as an undeniable Avatar of Truth, I am erecting a bulwark of direct existential experience that exposes the unconscionable violence against women that has run rampant in this town far too long." Manifesta adjusted the elongate holder once again and placed it, sans cigarette, between her lips.

"You certainly exposed something tonight. There is no denying that. I've never experienced anything like it in terms of unvarnished realism and my own visceral responses." I found myself wondering about the wellsprings of her inspiration. The majesty, the artistry, the exalted cinematography all had to have some serious kind of muse behind it, and I was beginning to realize why Zilch had given me this lead.

"Tonight, I exposed the cowardly male ego that hides behind celebrity, group psychology, sociological conventions, and male chauvinism while it denies a modern woman the dignity of her own free will. I also exposed Hollywood's hatred against women for what it is—violent and self-righteous envy of her liberated sexuality."

"I'm not sure I would go that far ..."

"No, of course you wouldn't, Mister Philosopher to the Stars, but someone has to! And apparently, that someone has to be a woman who knows what it's like to be a woman, a woman of passionate convictions and vision," she said as she carefully repositioned the eye-widening monocle within her eye socket. As Manifesta's passions flared, her entire countenance took on an increasingly appealing gleam. "I consider myself to be an artistic champion of justice," she said with an evocative flurry of her tresses. "And there has been no justice for beautiful women in this town, only exploitation, contempt, and violence. Where there is no justice, there is always violence! And I for one intend to bring this revelation of man's violence against women back into the streets!" Her cheeks flushed, her gaze intensified, and she virtually shimmered with a crimson hue.

"Bravo, Manifesta," I attempted to say, but she cut me off.

"I am creating a new myth for society—*the myth of the eternal rerun*—and I intend to rerun this violence against women again and again with increasing levels of realism until no one can escape the veracity of the direct physical experience." When she finished speaking, she leaned gracefully back, exposing an abundance of female pulchritude, fiery red flames set against the milky whiteness of the leather upholstery.

I couldn't help but wonder about her sexual orientation, considering the strident feminism she expounded. I concluded the following: if she was indeed a lesbian, she was definitely one of the most beautiful lesbians in the world.

"I clearly see ... ummm ... and understand the sociological value of a feminist provocateur," I said, attempting to find common ground from which to launch my next tack. "I happen to share your repugnance for exploitation and violence, as it is directed against women in Hollywood, and I consider myself to be an advocate of women's rights." Apparently, my wandering thoughts were transparent to her, for she leaned fully forward again, exposing the delectable fullness of two perfect breasts, and then she gave me a good hard mono-monocular squint.

"And would your responses be exactly the same if the dearly departed Ayn Rand were here in this same dress staring at you in the face?"

Suddenly, I was embarrassed by my own juxtaposition of the immediate eye-pleasing, mouth-watering beauty before me vis-à-vis the eternal beauty of the philosophical propositions under discussion. I was even more embarrassed when it occurred to me just how easy it was for me to use my powers of selective perception to obviate the objective reality while I made love to a headless Venus of Cyrene. Chastened by the revelation of my own constitutional weakness, I resorted to the last refuge of a Philosophical Counselor *in extremis*, that is, to surrender to a literal truth.

"I'm afraid I see your point all too well," I said. "I mean, I truly *see* your point. I am beginning to realize that any attempt to weasel my way out of this would be futile, and I would probably end up hating myself in the morning."

"Finally, a philosopher who refuses to argue against a painful reality—there might be some hope for mankind yet," she said, and then she dropped a bombshell. "Kaltrina Dahl and I both know why you wanted to meet with me this evening, and we both know who it is you're working for. Please come to our new home in the Pacific Palisades next Tuesday evening, and we'll tell you what you need to know."

As I was leaving, Manifesta handed me a large ripe red tomato with an address—freshly scripted with a Sharpie—on the surface of its otherwise flawless skin.

On my way out, I remembered that Scarlett was waiting for me at the bar.

"Anyone who endeavors to argue with your boss had best be prepared to lose," I said with an undeniable tincture of chagrin.

"Really, darling, how did it go?" asked Scarlett, slurping the remainder of her Bloody Mary.

"Frankly, Scarlett, I made a damn fool of myself," I admitted while fondling the tomato.

"Don't worry about it, handsome. I'm sure others have done much worse."

We hit the Strip sometime before midnight, and I gathered the Porsche from the valet guy at Mel's.

Scarlett flashed me that kind of smile that stays with a man, and she spoke with the supreme confidence of a real live angel: "Lucky you, Doctor Metropolis. You get to take me home."

7. Fall of the Bildungsroman Empire

As inspiration is the breath of the psyche, expiration is the dearth of philosophy. And I still didn't have a clue. For all my investigative epistemology, I had gained little if any ground teleologically. I myself was beginning to feel the requiem of death approaching, beginning to feel as if I was backed up in a dark corner, and I still didn't know who or what was eluding me. Sure, sure, I knew all about the function of the muse in literature and art and even tragedy. What I didn't know was how I was going to explain to Zilch that, while I had become somewhat sensitized to the depravity and causality of the deplorable act of murder, I had learned next to nothing about Kaltrina Dahl—other than that she had taken up with one of the most beautiful lesbians in the world who was now eating his lunch, cinematically. How do you explain something like that that to a man like Zilch who already knows that he is losing his luster?

I decided not to answer his calls until I had a better handle on the whys and wherefores of this case. Besides, I had my own troubles to consider. I was becoming increasingly attached to a hyperreal Hollywood starlet whose tragic fate was cruelly preordained in every theatrical sense. As a Philosophical Counselor, I had spent the greater part of my adult life reveling in the notion that mankind, properly nurtured and guided by sublime inspiration, has the potential to be supremely creative among all creatures. And now I find myself backed up into a dark corner, forced to examine the countervailing coercion of mankind—*the imp of the perverse*—that primal bestial instinct that betrays creative genius and plants the vile seeds of annihilation into the material and spiritual filaments of the cosmos. Like Edgar Allen Poe himself, I was being forced through love and loss to transcend the bounds of traditional morality and to search for the roots of this radical impulse that rules the dark side of human behavior.

Every time I looked at Scarlett, I saw the tragedy of Darla Darkcity. And try as I might, I couldn't separate the glamorous starlet that she wanted to be, the charming young woman whose expressions of vivacity and desire that she affectionately projected at me, from the immutable *fixité* of circumstance that reminds me of the extreme cruelty of fate, the unsightliness of death, and the lurking impulse of perversity that is tantamount to murder. Perhaps we were both being backed into a dark corner of the human condition: she by her feminine inclination to become the object of every man's desire and me by my perspicuous eye that sees the raiment of the Black Swan as a prelude to catastrophe.

Looming over the both of us, like the dreaded Sword of Damocles, was a specter of fear that attends such misfortune and my acute awareness of the *imp of the perverse*. This destructive counterpart to creativity, this primitive predisposition toward perversity, this unreasonable impulse which impels, this irresistible force which compels, this overwhelming tendency of people in privileged positions to do wrong for wrong's sake has become absolutely elementary in this town. This unfathomable longing of the soul of Hollywood to vex itself—to offer violence to own nature—to do wrong for wrong's sake only, to continue to consummate the injury it had inflicted upon the unoffending dream of beauty and thereby place itself beyond the reach of redemption; it tasks me.

Now, one might wax philosophical to the point of mythic detachment, where the bright and shining gods of the studios simply behave like boisterous children, much like the adolescent Phaethon (son of Helios and Clymene, the Titan goddess of renown, fame, and infamy) who tried to drive his father's sun-chariot but crashed, that is, after nearly setting fire to the whole earth. It is all very well and good to pontificate upon the frailty of human nature with the detachment of a modern politician capitalizing on the threat of global warming. But it's quite another thing entirely to look into the watering eyes of your newly beloved and realize that she has already chosen of her own free will to become the object of the compulsion of the perversity.

For Scarlett had purposefully placed herself at risk. By plotting and aspiring to be discovered, to ascend the heights of fame and fortune through an individual's adherence to an iconic appeal and, thus, one's marketable connections rather than laboring faithfully by more natural means, her demeanor represents a new form of hyperlative transcendentalism that has emerged with the postmodern production of music, mass media, and film. In the name of perennial beauty, artistry, philosophy, and nature itself, I reject such reductionist vanity, regardless of its financial connotations. It's shocking, I know. Sometimes I surprise myself. In a very real sense, I found myself attempting to hold the hideous specter of Darla's untimely death in abeyance.

Apparently, Poe's rejection of transcendental thinking was sorely misunderstood in his time, as well. So, as "*a way of mitigating the accusations*" that were made against him ... as "*a way of staying the execution,*" as it were, Poe offered a sanguine morality of his own by penning the "tale with a moral" entitled *Never Bet the Devil Your Head*. Alas, the implicit moral didacticism, which appeared in many small villages long before we were born, has unfortunately arrived in this town far too late. For nearly everyone who is anyone in Hollywood has already placed their bets.

. . .

Over the weekend, I found my usual underground parking space graced with a nearly-new azure blue Ferrari California. Pity the poor executive who crashed and burned with such a flourish as to make this repossession possible—for the good taste of a true automotive connoisseur should have counted for something. As it was, the Prancing Horse and I needed to get better acquainted. I needed to get a good feel for the more intimate driving pleasures at hand and to try, at the very least, to take the top down on a first date. Thankfully, the Pacific Coast Highway and the Southern California weather are amenable to the point of encouraging such brief yet intimate romances on the road.

On Tuesday afternoon, I took the extended southern route to the Pacific Palisades, catching the bliss and the pendulous sunset down around Dana Point, pawing and clutching the lithe mechanical tintinnabulum while spewing open air music along the gentle curves of Newport Beach, redressing the elegant convertible hardtop once again at Surfside, while straining with only minor indignities through the denser patches of rush hour traffic at Sepulveda past the LA

International Airport and emerging renewed along a stretch of the Santa Monica coastline with my latest automotive relationship fully and satisfyingly consummated.

The lush green of the Santa Monica Mountains and the sandy beaches of the Pacific Ocean had surrendered fully to darkness by the time I approached the high bluffs of the Palisades, home of the original Getty Museum, the Self-Realization Fellowship Lake Shrine, and the recherché of the movie business. Swerving passed a ravine that serves as the entrance to the gardens of the Lake Shrine, I was reminded of a previous client of mine—a particularly unfortunate individual who had gone to all the trouble to break into the Chinese sarcophagus that held a significant portion of Mahatma Ghandi's ashes, with the intention of holding said ashes for ransom. The most unfortunate thing for my client was that fact that no one in all of Los Angeles was the least bit interested in paying the ransom. I was able to assist this client in abating the understandable levels of deep depression and self-loathing that he experienced in the aftermath of his failed extortion attempt, and I did so by introducing some scintillating embers of Hindu philosophy as part of this patient's court-ordered mental rehabilitation. But I was never able to convince him to tell me exactly what he did with, or rather, where he had hidden, Mahatma Ghandi's ashes. Some truths remain elusive even unto philosophy.

When I arrived at the specified residence on Paseo Miramir, the scene was bathed in the soft glow of many meticulously placed spotlights, calmly illuminating the landscape as well as the exposed beams, hardwoods, and glass of the modernist hillside gem. The front door had been left open several inches, which I assumed was for me to enter *ad libitum*—which I quietly proceeded to do. The open-space layout of the post and beam structure emphasized a horizontal composition, much like a frame of movie film, with linear beams, walls of glass, and vast expanses of varnished ceilings. The floors were as black as that director's clapboard, a continuum of obsidian tiles punctuated by the placement of beige modern furniture amongst a few tables of stainless steel and glass. A refined minimalism was apparent everywhere you looked, creating a play of space and light and panoramic views. The only thing missing was any sign of my hosts, but then I was already busy enjoying the unobstructed views of Los Angeles after dark.

From another angle of the cliff-side perch, I could view the Santa Monica coastline, and I was wondering if I could see the lights of Catalina Island in the distance when I saw something move in the foreground, out of the corner of my eye. Emerging in a sudden ill-lit flash from the swimming pool that was nested in the natively planted hillside, and then disappearing into the darkness by the near side of the building, I saw what appeared to be either a very delicate woman or a very large swan. Before I could clarify my observation by following the creature's wet footsteps on the surrounding patio floor, I was greeted by the sound of Manifesta's distinctively directorial voice behind me.

"It would be better if you come and sit over here by the fire." Indeed, there was a fire in what appeared to be a sitting area, a flickering fire in high definition on a large flat panel display.

"Better for what?" I asked, continuing to look out the window in hopes of seeing the curious figure again. "I was beginning to enjoy the view."

"Better for us to talk, Doctor Metropolis. Better for us to talk about Zero Vaynilovich for one thing. Better for us to talk about Kaltrina Dahl for another."

I turned to face Manifesta. She was wearing tight black jeans and a black T-shirt that only accentuated what it was meant to obscure. She motioned for me to take a seat in one of the beige lounge chairs while she seated herself, *splendidly* I must say, in another.

"Wasn't that Kaltrina Dahl I just saw climbing out of the swimming pool? And were those feathers she was wearing?"

"Kaltrina may join us later, depending on how she feels."

"Okay, if you say so. I'm just happy that you agreed to see me again … on behalf of my client, of course."

"Of course," she said in reply.

I noticed that Manifesta still had the empty cigarette holder, which she adjusted and placed between her lips from time to time, but she was not sporting the monocle this evening. Considering the possibility—the sheer, the remote, the almost ridiculous possibility that the monocle, of all things, may have something to do with the lost, or stolen, yet clearly missing object in question—that this object of auspicious attire that adorned the eye sockets of such famous filmmakers as Fritz Lang and Erich von Stroheim and which served as a metaphor for the literary avant-garde, a status symbol for the upper crust, a ring of power for the politicians, and a focus of authority for everyone from military tyrants to well-dressed dummies, could be it! Could this *objective singularity* really represent the object of poor Zilch's desire? I had to ask.

"I noticed that you aren't wearing a monocle this evening?"

"You mean *the* monocle. And no, I only wear it when I create my Art."

"Is that so," I said rhetorically. I eased up, but I was far from satisfied.

"Yes, Doctor Metropolis, it is so. And you can ask me anything you like about my artistic creations, but nothing will be gained by probing into my personal effects."

"Well, one part of my commission is to gain access to the actual source of your inspiration, artistically speaking, that is." I knew that I was on shaky ground, so I quickly shifted my approach. "I was wondering, etiologically, that is, if you share any origins or developmental continuities with that fellow Kristophales. You know, that guy who goes around covering things up with curtains, ostensibly in an effort to *reveal* them. Isn't that fellow engaged in manifesting the same kind of Public Art as you are?"

"Oh, please! You disappoint me, philosophically speaking, that is," she said, not only parrying my provocative thrust, but completely uncovering my ruse. And now that I was exposed to her contempt, as a poor player, so to speak, she focused her attention on my codpiece, as it were.

"Don't even think about grouping me, my source of inspiration, or my Art with that machismo miscreant! We have absolutely nothing in common!" Once again, Manifesta's womanly visage appeared to glow more brightly with the elevation of her tenor. "You, of all people, should be able to look into the origins of *his* inspiration as easily as a Freudian psychotherapist can look into the developmental psychology of a hysteric." Her momentary frown was a perfect portrait of her disapproval. "And if you bothered to do so, you would see the male perversity that is at its base. You would see, in his early works, the attempts to constrain the female figure—the binding ropes, the high tensile fabrics, the intricate knots—the obvious sadist aesthetic should be as clear to you as the so-called artistry of Japanese bondage pornography!"

She had me there, for there were certain aspects of an essential inferiority complex to be discerned, an inkling of an inferiority complex that seeks to assert some grandiose control over greater works of art and architecture and even nature, in all its glory, in all its feminine nurturing aspects, by an inescapable act or shroud of man's domination. Indeed, Manifesta had me backed up into that same proverbial dark corner, and I had no idea of what she was going to hit me with next. I decided to take it like a man.

"And as far as Public Art goes, there is no comparison!" she declared. "If you bothered to think before you speak, you would have realized that the true *modus operandi* of Kristophales and his kind, and by this I mean modern man's obsession to wreak havoc upon the most sacred of monuments, takes place behind the scenes. The intense and aggressive undercurrent of social complicity, where everything is executed in complete compliance with the local authorities as the political artist dutifully navigates the bureaucratic systems surrounding these intended victimization projects, as he negotiates, at length in the face of repeated rejections in a characteristically manic pursuit, which elevates the diagnosis of base desire to that of an obsession, as well as a compulsion."

Manifesta paused for a moment, adjusting the length of the cigarette holder, and then she continued on with her speech.

"Even the lamest of the psychoanalytical practitioners would have to agree that the obsessive repetitions of the political machinations reveal the truly aggressive nature of Kristophales' work. The overwrought cartographic depictions, the militaristic surveillance of the victim, the working models designed for show-and-tell all correlate with the obsessive nature of a pursuit for permission. But low and behold, this is not the bona fide permission of either the original artist or the grand architect, but from the complicit circles of the political, social, and capitalistic *good old boys* in whose neighborhoods this despicable Public Art will be displayed. Ultimately, all the *good old boys* get to live out their domineering fantasies in public, but they do so to the detriment of femininity itself."

"I sometimes feel exactly the same way." I had no idea where I was going with this, but I had to try and stop this train before it ran me over completely. "I also find myself emotionally set against the victimization of the female, as it is generally, historically, and often tragically played out in this town."

"Well then, why not philosophically, Mister Philosopher to the Stars? What are you waiting for?" she said with biting indignation. "Why is there still not one iota of real feminism to be dreamt of in your philosophy? Don't you realize yet that this is the very crux of the matter, the crux of the matter that you have been sent like an errand-boy to find, the crux of the matter that defines the very essence of the creativity that Zero Vaynilovich now lacks?"

"I thought we were talking about Kristophales, or are we done with that guy?" I tried to avert my gaze to the faux fire burning sedately in the flat-screen fireplace, but to no avail, for my attention was drawn back to the shimmering intensity of the woman.

"Not quite," she declared. "Not until you understand the male aggressor as I do and the target of violence as I do … can you or anyone else even begin to see the true nature of the hostile commentary at work—the hostile commentary that I oppose by my own work in socially responsible cinematography with an equal and opposite force!"

There was no doubt about it. Manifesta was the intellectual equal of any man, equally superior in every way. The dramatic means by which she manifested and indeed defended her socially responsible snuff films, it left me agog. It was all I could do to keep up with her magnificent thoughts while my head nodded repeatedly, like a plastic figurine in the rear window of an old beat-up muscle car.

"From a truly creative point of view," she continued, "Kristophales' entire oeuvre of monumental and environmental kitsch simply reeks of the obsessive compulsive behavior of an insecure male monad, rank with vile adolescent impulses that arise—much to the offense of my artistic eye—from the miserable Bildungsroman of the male gonad. And this entire oeuvre of dubious Public Art stands—as it is, as it were, as it always will be—diametrically opposed to the final liberation and the emergence of the creative, decisive woman of the twenty-first century."

Manifesta had barely moved within her beige lounge chair, except to adjust and reinsert the empty cigarette holder on occasion. And I had barely moved, except to nod my head up and down like a fool. Still, I felt as if I had just been through a battle of sorts, replete with Ninja warriors and Kung Fu fighting. It was exhausting and somewhat sad to lose such a match, but sadder still if I failed to find something of value that might serve to recoup the unbearable sadness and the tangible losses of my client, the *Latest Tycoon.*

"If I affirm the emendatory criticism of the gifted female provocateur, does the errand-boy receive a small gratuity to bring back to the grocery clerk?" I was attempting to reaffirm the formal assertion that humor, like anger, is more useful than despair.

"You amuse me, Doctor Metropolis, and that's quite rare in this business."

"Isn't it time you called me Joe?" I asked, hoping to bridge the gender gap.

"I really don't think so. While I do sense certain redeeming qualities in your absence of malice and your general presence of mind, it is my experience with men that such familiarity invariably breeds contempt."

As we were posturing, a most delicate, attractive, and arresting voice of a woman literally floated into the room.

"Now, now, Manifesta, the man did ask you nicely, even humbly, in my opinion. He has managed to endure your caustic diatribe, and he deserves the same respect from you that you would ask of him." It was obviously—as I had hoped and expected—the voice of the elusive Kaltrina Dahl. Everything I had heard about her seemed to fit with the faultless elocution. The soft, cool voice-over came from beyond the patio, but there was no Kaltrina Dahl in sight.

I rose from my chair, more from habit than chivalry, and started to walk toward the outdoor pool. Manifesta rose also, more elegantly than I, of course, as if in response, but she simply stood without moving, her graceful arms crossed with impatience beneath her lovely breasts. But before I reached the actual opening in the plate glass wall, established by the wide-open position of the sliding glass doors, the voice-over implored me to halt with a perceptible note of urgency:

"Please stop, Doctor Metropolis. Please don't try and come any farther." Kaltrina's voice was still soft and cool. The room was still clear and bright, but she was not there.

"Why in the world not?" I asked in protest, but I stopped in my tracks just the same.

"She is afraid that you'll fall in love with her," said Manifesta, immediately and unequivocally. I turned to face Manifesta out of sheer curiosity. "They always do," she added with a note of disapproval while slowly shaking her head.

"Is that true, Kaltrina? Is that why you don't want me to see you in person?"

There was no answer, only a soft rustling in the darkness. When it was clear that no direct answer would be forthcoming, Manifesta spoke with indignation. "Modesty forbids," was all she said.

I myself remained dumbfounded, standing alone in the center of the room.

It was really strange to have a conversation with the disembodied muse, but it served my purpose well enough. Speaking to me from the darkness, as though it were the "fourth wall" of a theatrical stage, Kaltrina explained to me the historical romance behind her ethereal fondness for Zilch, extending her guileless appreciation to the many excellent motion pictures they made together, while Manifesta grew increasingly impatient. I was amazed by the elevation of purpose that was magnified by her cultivated discourse and the inspiring leaven with which her enlightened intentions were portrayed. There was an alluring quality about Kaltrina Dahl—there was no sense in denying that. The word *enchantment* comes to mind.

"I need to ask you about a stolen object, Kaltrina. I don't mean to offend or accuse, but it has been related to me in those terms by Zero Vaynilovich, and he seems to want this stolen object back rather badly … in addition to your affections, of course."

"You can tell dear Zero that I know all too well what it is that he wants. But I am also acutely aware of what it is that he currently lacks."

Waxing Aristotelian, I suggested some form of compromise in an effort to moderate the discord, as a desirable attribute of beauty, as an approach to restoring harmony. I suggested that Kaltrina meet personally with Zilch to talk things over, but all I got, from near and far, was the unmitigated silence of the crypt.

"If you insist on asserting the utility of your philosophical imperatives, I will tell you," said Kaltrina Dahl finally in a thoroughly declarative voice. "The very thing that he truly needs will arrive via the Metrolink train, heading down-bound for Los Angeles, and he can find it there two weeks from tomorrow at precisely six o'clock in the morning at the Glendale train station. Now, if you will excuse me, it's time for me to change into my evening attire and get ready for bed."

"I'd say it's been nice meeting you…" I said sarcastically, "but since we haven't actually met yet, I'll just say that it's hard to say good-bye."

"Truer words have never been spoken," said Manifesta with an equal measure of sarcasm. "Now if there isn't anything more I can do for you, I'm feeling rather tired myself." She feigned a yawn with the graceful aplomb of a Russian prima ballerina and spun around ever so slowly to show me the door.

"Well, if it wouldn't be too much trouble … that is, if you could bear to do me the favor … I mean, if you could find it in your heart to tell me more about your current work in contemporary film. You see, I am not only interested in helping out with the sorrows of Zero Vaynilovich, but I am becoming more and more interested in your hyperreal cinematography, your fixation on unrequited Hollywood murders, and your obvious passion for women's liberation."

"Oh, please. If you promise not to lump me together with my simple-minded, bra-burning sisters who came and went like a swarm of fireflies in the night," she said as she stretched the expanses and the blackness of her T-shirt with another exaggerated yawn. And then proceeded to plop herself back into the beige lounge chair—only this time, her shapely legs were crossed one over the other in those jet black jeans, and one of them began ticking away like a metronome set on high speed.

.   .   .

I met with Manifesta again, by personal invitation, two days later on location. She was busy with a production crew assembling booms and reflectors and assorted high-tech paraphernalia at a place in downtown

LA called Angels Flight. Billed as "The World's Shortest Railway," the steeply inclined tracks once connected the original downtown shopping district with the financial district atop Bunker Hill. The grade is so steep that the two railway cars had to be specially fabricated on an angle and counterbalanced by a cable to operate on such an angle, but the whole operation was closed down after a fatal accident many years ago. As of now, the original railroad cars are in storage, waiting for the promise of a renovation that has never come. In this town, the prevailing mantra is always "Coming Soon."

Manifesta's crew was setting up shop in the open-air plaza at the top of the railroad platform amidst an urban setting of fountains and ponds. I found her stationed near the top of the tracks on a narrow walkway in front of the original Victorian gateway. She was wearing the same tight black jeans, with black leather boots, but the black T-shirt had been replaced by the exquisite sheerness of black chiffon. It appeared that she was using lasers to calculate a number of exacting measurements from the tracks to various angles and objective locales. When I got close enough to see her face, I noticed that she was wearing the conspicuous monocle.

"Thanks for allowing me the pleasure of watching an upcoming Hollywood film director at work," I said, leaning over the railing.

"As long as you don't confuse me with the other directors or producers in this town, I'll allow you to stay." Manifesta stopped what she was doing and climbed up to the railing so she wouldn't have to shout. "You know that I'm nothing like them, and I don't ever want to be. You shouldn't presume that I want to break some kind of glass ceiling for the sake of sexism. I no more want to join the male-dominated Director's Guild than I would want to break into the male-dominated syndicates of crack dealers. Sexism is simply not my style—in fact, I find the subject rather uninteresting."

"How can you separate your radical brand of feminism from the trappings of sexism? Aren't they two sides of the same coin?"

"Hardly," she said, her feminine voice advancing against the sounds of the oblivious city. "I do not intend to blaze a path that other, lesser individuals can easily follow. I admire leaders, not followers, no matter their sex," she declared, raising her laser pointer skyward. "And it will take leaders with vision and indomitable courage to challenge the prevailing macho aristocracy and to encourage children of the future to assert their own will to power. With my work in digital compositing and my cinematic Art, I raise the bar higher than it ever was before, with the challenge and the warning to man and woman alike—that the *Charites*, the great goddesses of beauty and creativity, favor the most deserving."

"I assume you are referring to the *Gratiae*, or Graces, in Roman terms. Aren't these Charites or Graces closely associated with the Muses?" I smoothly inquired. As a Philosophical Counselor on the job, I do have my moments.

"Absolutely," was all she said as she descended the platform to adjust some arcane electronic equipment. Then she beamed a laser light across the tracks to a particular point on the side of an adjacent building.

I watched in silence for quite a while with increasing amazement at the elegance and the efficiency of her movements, the concentration of her intents and purposes, the remarkable albeit subliminal communications with her co-workers whose activities were in obvious concordance—like an inscrutable anthill of laborers at work or rather like so many busy bees in the service of their queen. The degree of mastery and discipline and focus of each and every technician was impressive to say the least, while all around us on the visible streetscapes, the streams of traffic, the streams of pedestrians, the airliners streaming overhead created a veritable symphony of obliviousness, all completely ignorant to the latent industry of her Art.

I waited patiently for Manifesta to finish what she was doing. It was past midday when she joined me on the granite steps that surround the gurgling fountains.

"May I ask what kind of spectacle you are creating here, Manifesta?"

"If you promise to tell no one in advance," she said, expectant of my oath. Her sheer blouse, glistening with iridescent sequins of perspiration, clung to her curves as tightly as her jeans.

"I promise to keep your secret from all but two, the first being my client."

"No problem. Zero Vaynilovich is too proud to even recognize my work, let alone interfere." She signaled for her minions to carry on without her with a fluttering wave of her hand. "And who is this second person that you simply must inform?"

"Actually, she is one of yours, but I don't think she is involved in this project. Her name is Scarlett, your body double for Darla Darkcity. Would you mind terribly if I shared this cinematic event with her?"

"Oh, she already knows. They all do. Everyone in the artistic avant-garde is intimately connected, don't you know? And Scarlett, the brave girl, will always be welcome by my lamplights."

The reflections in the water court shimmered with the passing breezes. I caught a momentary softness in Manifesta's eyes as she spoke of Scarlett. I searched for that soft spot as I confessed, "I'm not sure that I can bear to watch the spectacle that you have in store for her. I'm not certain that I can even bear the thought."

"But that's precisely the point, Doctor Metropolis."

An airliner passed over the city, descending toward LAX in the background.

"I know. I know. I realize all too well the tragic necessity of your work. And I truly admire the courage and conviction it takes to confront and expose the ugly truths behind the privileges of this town that perpetually harbors such abuse. It's just that the degree of realism you create is so unnerving, and I am becoming so fond of Scarlett personally, as she is, that I am not at all certain that I could even bear to watch the scene of her murder."

Manifesta smiled—an expression that was almost impish, but not entirely dismissive. "Silly Rabbit," she quipped, "my Trix are for your kids!"

I all but swooned as the brilliance of a finer future flashed before my eyes. I felt an invisible skein of stardust falling faintly through the universe and faintly falling, like the descent of that final curtain, on all the living dead.

Manifesta went on to describe the new project she had in mind for Angel's Flight. Based on the stereotype of the *Damsel in Distress*, designed to raise and destroy the concept of the helpless female, she was preparing to project, cinematically, a number of famous starlets onto the rails of the declivitous tracks—illusively, holographically, and hyperrealistically—like phantoms in the night, while she and her production crew filmed the emotional responses of the unwitting spectators with her high-definition, high-tech motion picture cameras hidden in the antique station houses. Her *treatment* of the illusory corpses gave me the creeps. Still, I wouldn't miss it for the world.

8. Magnificent Intemperate Impulses

It was time for me to face Zero Vaynilovich. I couldn't put it off any longer. I had gained just enough information to make it interesting, but not enough for him or me or anyone else to act upon. It's hard to face a man named Zilch when all you've got is nothing.

"Let me get this straight. You've been on the job for two weeks, and all you've got to show for yourself are two dead bodies, a disfigured statue, eyewitness accounts of an unsolved murder, shaky evidence of a second murder plot, accusations of a serial sadist on the loose, and rumors of famous starlets scheduled to be tied to a railroad track?"

"Yes, that's about it."

"Some kinda detective you are." Zilch stormed about his office as if he were putting out a brush fire. In Hollywood, offices are more than offices. For movie-studio executives, the size, grandeur, and accessories of the setup where one holds court is a map to status and a key to the subtleties of local politics. Judging from the size of the place, the anteroom with two exceedingly attractive secretaries, the herringbone patterns on the exotic hardwood floors, the antique furniture, the conference table bedecked with Wedgewood china, and the exquisite executive desk built on top of a platform—not to mention the working fireplace of gold-veined black marble and the private bathroom off in the distance—Zilch obviously had ordered the studio to spend as much money as possible on his office, thus emphasizing his value.

"But Mister Zilch, I'm not a detective, and I never advertised myself as such. I am a Philosophical Counselor, and you engaged me to—"

"I know why the hell I engaged you, Metropolis. It's just that I'm desperate, and I was expecting something more from you, something more insightful perhaps."

"Well, I did have a brief Socratic dialogue with Kaltrina Dahl in which she expressed interest in your work and discussed your previous relationship. Moreover, I encouraged her to meet with you in person in an attempt to find some middle ground."

"You mean you actually saw her?" he asked as he mounted the platform to his desk.

"Well, not actually," I said, taking my seat in a leather club chair.

"What do you mean *not actually*? Did you see her or didn't you?"

"Before I try and answer that, could you tell me if she likes to wear feathers?"

"Why, yes," he said, shuffling casually through some papers. "She certainly does."

"Does she wear these feathers all the time?"

"No. Not at nighttime, of course." He stopped shuffling. "What are you getting at?"

"Then I do think I saw her. Yes, I saw her briefly, that is."

"Well, if you saw her briefly, how in the world did you manage to have a conversation with her about our relationship and our prospective reconciliation?"

"I think you would call it voice-over."

"And where was the nouveau notorious Manifesta when you were having this voice-over conversation with my Dahlia?" The crumpling of the papers with the clenching of his fists was clearly more dramatic than it was threatening. "And if you tell me how beautiful this presumed lesbian is one more time, I'll ... I'll ... I'll ...."

I knew that Zilch was reaching the limits of his tether, so I offered him some prescient philosophical advice: "*All beings hitherto have created something beyond themselves—as you have with your films—and ye want to be the ebb of that great tide.* The only question you need to answer at this moment is this: *Would you rather go back to the beast than surpass the man?*"[17]

---

17   Nietzsche, in *Thus Spake Zarathustra*.

"I would rather have my Kaltrina back. With her, I could surpass the lesbian!" His clenched fists came down hard upon the executive desk.

"Indeed," was all I could say. I was acutely aware of the gaping maw of emptiness that Zilch was facing, an emptiness that roared with a terrifying ferocity. For Zilch, reality itself was an endless epoch of becoming, a gaining of power with the industrious creation of each masterful illusion. Throughout his life as a writer and director and producer of films, he had erected a sober and rational and active principle dedicated to the creation of an Apollonian spell, "*Now Showing in Theaters Everywhere.*" But now, he was forced to witness the cinematographic revelation of human nature in all its naked actuality, with all its unconscious, involuntary, overwhelmingly self-destructive instincts, culminating in a Dionysian frenzy that threatens to destroy all previous forms and codes. The fact that his beloved muse is part and parcel of this brave new wave of high-tech, hyperreal cinematography makes the return to Dionysian actuality even more painful.

"Look here, Mister Zilch. I'm just beginning to get a handle on this case, which, as I recall, was focused on the *motive* for Kaltrina Dahl's departure. I have gained certain insights from both Byron Harmsway, may he rest in peace, and Kaltrina Dahl herself. However, I am not sufficiently informed as to offer you a working hypothesis at this point. I believe it may come down to the underlying values, ideals, and attitudes you hold dear, and I promise that, if you give me the time to approach Kaltrina Dahl on her own terms, I will get to the philosophical rock bottom of this mystery."

"Your search for answers sure takes a long time. But what other choice have I got?" His head and body slumped, indicating to me that he was resigned to defeat.

"There is one more thing, Mister Zilch. Kaltrina told me to tell you that the very thing you are missing the most would be on the morning train to Los Angeles next Wednesday morning and that you would be able find what you're looking for at the railway station in Glendale at six o'clock."

"Why didn't you say so before?" said Zilch, brightening as with the dawn. "This is exactly what I've been waiting for. It may not be the love of my life, but it's a step in the right direction. I'll pick you up at your seedy office on my way to the Glendale station. Meanwhile, I expect you to work on solving the case of my lost love every waking hour. And I want you to know that *time is of the essence!*"

. . .

I was working every angle of the case, including the theory that "*art is the mimesis of nature.*"[18] I had managed to get myself invited back to Manifesta's home for further discussions of her aesthetics by elaborating on my interest in the birth of tragedy and the latest developments in catharsis theory, but our next meeting remained to be formally scheduled. In the meantime, I decided to give Scarlett a call, this time for personal reasons—at least my own motivations were perfectly clear.

Scarlett told me to meet her and some friends at the Wax Museum on Hollywood Boulevard, which is open 365 days a year from 10 AM to midnight. It's located near the refurbished Hollywood & Highland Center, where tourists tend to congregate in chorus; the Grauman's Chinese Theater, where the most admired petroglyphs are constantly underfoot; and the El Capitan, where real, live Disney characters reaffirm Lord Byron's dictum that "*Truth is always strange; stranger than fiction, if it could be told.*"[19]

But *truth* is never told outright in this particular town. It is sometimes hidden. It is often distorted. It is bent and battered and beaten to a pulp. It is focused on vaguely. It is diffused like light. It is rendered and dismembered all over town. It is modeled. It is suggested. It is implicit and implied. It is never told, but it is sometimes hinted at, like the gleam in a mannequin's eye.

On the corner of the block, there was a life-size replica of a Tyrannosaurus Rex sticking up out of a building. The creature was holding a clock in its mouth as if to remind me of Zilch's timely imperative. I was instead reminded of a particular Latin phrase inscribed over the doorway of Carl Jung's house and again upon his

---

18   A Greek idea, developed in Plato's *Republic* and Aristotle's *Poetics*.
19   Lord Byron's poem *Don Juan*.

tomb; it is a phrase that harkens the reader to the eternal within the present: *Vocatus atque non vocatus, Deus aderit*—summoned or not, the gods will come—a note of the eternal regardless of the intent. The sign outside the Hollywood Wax Museum presages a similar haunting, but by considerably less distinguished guests. I, for one, was in search of an angel.

Inside among the darkness and the shadowy curtains stood silent scads of waxen celebrities who once strutted and fretted their waning hours upon the silver screen, telling their tales of times gone by and futures yet to come. There were hundreds of figures of historic melodrama and bombast all caught within the same macabre envelopes of low-key lighting, as were the most contemporary of celebrities. With the exception of an occasional shriek or a blurted bolus of laughter echoing from the adjacent Chamber of Horrors, the entire dwelling was nearly deserted.

I was beginning to wonder if I should go back outside again to wait for Scarlett and her friends when I saw the grim visage of Darla Darkcity standing motionless on the grand staircase. Gazing at her likeness from headshot to high heels, I was gripped by a vile specter of malevolence along with a painful reminder that my lovely Fourth-Order Simulacrum, my beauteous *Angel of the Hyperreal* was tragically, voluntarily doomed—that is, until I noticed that the statuesque figure was moving perceptibly, like a palm tree on a windy day. Pretending not to notice the prevailing sway, I moved in rather closely, as if to examine the more interesting aspects of the female anatomy.

"Don't make me laugh while I'm method acting." The whispered voice was thrown like a ventriloquist to its dummy.

"I was just admiring your costume, among other things," I whispered back. "The only thing wrong with your methods, from my point of view, is that there is no one else here but me to enjoy them."

"That makes no difference to me in the least," she said in a somewhat louder and noticeably more indignant whisper. "A true actress can perform just the same, regardless of the circumstances."

I looked around the ill-lit room and nodded. She was obviously playing to a full house. Still, I could not imagine that it would be the most appreciative of audiences.

Just then, there was a minor commotion in the adjacent room along with the sound of many loud voices all talking at once.

"Hush now. Don't you dare give me away," came the ventriloquist's whispered warning.

The vociferous sounds of men's voices drew nearer, and a retinue of business men in well-tailored suits began to enter the proscenium stage. Soon the room was virtually filled with a boisterous gaggle of mulling executives. The juxtaposition of the back-slapping jocularity, the notable designer labels, and the general vulgarity of their tasteless dialogues convinced me that the approaching gaggle was one of assistant Hollywood movie producers. While Scarlett, as Darla Darkcity, was busy with her method acting, it was all I that could do to act nonchalant.

"Kiss me now," I thought I heard Scarlett say to me in a whisper.

And of course, I would have jumped at the chance. But to be sure, I just looked my lovely body double straight in the eye and shrugged with quiet curiosity.

"Kiss me quick," she whispered again, and this time I heard her clearly.

Still, I was torn between the magnificent intemperate impulses of desire and the mandate not to disappoint the dramatic plotting of my statuesque femme fatale. "I don't understand," was all I could safely say at this most critical point in the play.

"What part of **Kiss me** don't you understand?" Scarlett said in a voice that was almost loud enough to be overheard.

Like an actor who has just realized that he missed his cue, I embraced the nearly motionless mannequin with the abandon of a jailbird on parole, and I began to kiss her on her mouth and her neck and her capacious breasts like a teenager at a drive-in movie. Reveling in the dizzying delights of my belated role as Scarlett's leading man, I had failed to notice the subtle yet hugely significant fact that the imperious mannequin was not kissing me back in the least perceptible degree. What I did notice was the fact that two of the waxy Keystone Cops on the staircase had suddenly come to life and were proceeding to escort me from the stage, rather roughly I might add, as they gave me the bum's rush all the way out into the street.

When I endeavored to ascertain exactly what in heaven's name the Keystone Cops were thinking, or more precisely, what they were doing, they were kind enough to offer me a perfectly rational explanation: "We're helping Scarlett to get discovered, and you were really great as the fall guy." And then they disappeared back into the Wax Museum, leaving me alone with the horror of my own realization.

Every nerve and sinew in my body, every active corpuscle of my blood, every fiber of my being was trembling as I realized that there was nothing I could do to stop the inevitable tragedy that was playing out before me, nothing I could do to oppose the seductive scenario that repeats itself over and over again on the seamy boulevards of this town, nothing I could do to resist the cruelty of fate exemplified by the hope-filled life and brutal death of the late Darla Darkcity. Perhaps if I were a better man, I would be able to take the woman in my arms and convince her not to go there.

.   .   .

Friday evening, I found myself attending the civic-minded snuff film I so dreaded. This time, the scene of the reenacted crime was at the corner of Wilshire and Westwood, a location where the obtuse angles of the competing office buildings create an arena not unlike Times Square in Manhattan. The crowd gathered as before, blocking traffic on both of the main thoroughfares and filling the entire intersection and the sidewalks from wall to wall. I noticed that yellow police tape had been strategically placed to heighten the sensations of the spectators at the scene of a crime. The news helicopters circling overhead did nothing to diminish the rising expectations.

I came alone, hoping against hope that I might be wrong, hoping that I might hear that assuring voice that that was meant only for me, hoping that I might feel that reassuring hand to hold and that amiable presence by my side, hoping that I might spend one more night in the arms of an angel. But I wasn't wrong. And hoping is not the stuff of philosophy. Neither is wishful thinking. Scarlett was somewhere in the crowd with her new assistant movie producer, and somehow, I just knew it. I didn't even have to see it. Pessimism is exceedingly reliable when it comes to human nature. Either way, I was destined to be the fall guy. And the sooner I realized that, the better.

The real live *Death of Darla Darkcity* at the hands of the deranged music producer was vivid, to be sure; it was grizzly and shocking and more horrifying than anyone could have imagined. What's more, it was real, more real than any previously scripted, carefully plotted, artfully directed, pretentiously acted, masterfully edited film ever was or is likely to be. At the point of the gun and the threat of the killing shot, it was as if the entire audience was frozen with fear, unable to move, unable to protest, unable to suspend their disbelief in the concept of evil for even an instant, as they were held captive by the palpable realism of the holography, riveted by the nails of direct experience, assailed by the virtual sounds of silence pulsating in their ears, while all illusions of a happy ending were literally blasted to smithereens by the explosion of their own hyperrealities. For me, it was the desolation of an angel, the very thing I dreaded most. And now it was even worse, for Scarlett was no longer on my arm to assure me that it wasn't real.

I have to admit, it was a masterpiece of social commentary. In the weeks to come, Manifesta would be the talk of the town. News of her recondite renderings of reality would spread around the world. Her new wave cinéma vérité would eventually have its day. Society at large would be duly disturbed. There would be trials and retrials, reminiscent of the days of Fatty Arbuckle. One person's vision would become the mandate of the people—dumb, panicky, and dangerous as they are—there would be a new demand for wide-eyed justice in the streets. Digital reduplications of Manifesta's artistic efforts would sell by the millions, along with holographic T-shirts and other Hollywood memorabilia. She would become a veritable "phenom" in this town and a legend in her own time. But tonight, as the crowd disbursed and disappeared into the LA cityscape, all that was but a dream to come, for I was alone with my thoughts of Scarlett and Darla Darkcity, as alone as anyone can be.

I bought a pack of Marlboro cigarettes from a Westwood convenience store and started looking for a place to smoke. I hardly smoke at all anymore—it just makes me dizzy and it makes my chest hurt, but I was feeling dead inside already and I needed a dark corner to complete the picture, the picture of the movie in my mind. Actually, I was looking for a scene I remembered from long ago. A scene from *One Lonely Night* when Mickey Spillane's Mike Hammer is walking alone on a rain-slicked city street, a night when it is good to be alone, a night when the cars hiss by with steamed-up windows, a night when you can walk and bury your head in the collar of your raincoat and pull the night around you like a blanket, a night when you can smoke and flip the spent butts ahead of you and watch them arch to the pavement and fizzle out with one last wink.

But it hardly ever rains in Southern California, until it does. And even then, no one wears raincoats. On a late summer night in Southern California, the metaphor of a blanket is the furthest thing from anyone's mind. But I did find the right place to smoke eventually. And I found myself alone on a night like this, or rather, that. I smoked the Marlboro cigarette, and then I flipped the spent butt ahead of me, and I watched it arch to the pavement. But instead of fizzling out with one last wink of noir, it just sparked and lay there on the asphalt, staring up at me in the darkness. I walked over to investigate and I saw that the glowing head of the cigarette had been dislodged from the shaft, and it lay there before me like a memento, a dying ember of an angel that was gradually disappearing from my sight.

.   .   .

I met Zilch in his limo on our way to the Glendale station. He had his driver fetch me from my office, which I considered rather impersonal, but then the driver handed me a cup of steaming hot coffee from Starbucks, and I was forced to reconsider my opinion. In his own way, Zilch had style.

"Are you certain she said that it would be on the 6 AM train?" asked Zilch.

"I'm certain about the time, the place, and the train," I said. "But I can't say that I am certain about the nature of either the subject or the indefinite object."

"Leave that to me. I told you it was personal, and it is ... very."

"Would you like me to explain what I've learned about the new wave of reality-based cinematography Manifesta is developing?" I queried, trying to make myself useful.

"I'm in the movie business, Metropolis. I can't afford any acute bouts of reality."

We rode the rest of the way to the train station in silence, sipping Starbucks through the slits in the artfully crafted lids.

It was early morning rush hour when the limo arrived at the station. The Pacific Surfliner and the Metrolink commuter trains were running pretty much on schedule. Amtrak's Surfliner trains that run from San Luis Obispo to San Diego, and vice versa, were all scheduled to arrive later in the morning, so it was the commuter trains that became the focus of our attention. At 6 AM, Zilch was busy pacing the walkway of the newly renovated California mission-style station, gazing intently, even expectantly, up and down the railroad tracks, while the driver was busy parking the limo in a space beyond the Greyhound buses. I was about to comment to Zilch on the perfectly flawless qualities of this establishing shot of *"business as usual"* on the outskirts of Los Angeles when I noticed a sport utility vehicle that had curiously stopped upon the tracks.

It simply stopped ... on the tracks ... as in stasis.

There are no other words to describe it. When Charles Marsh said that *"stasis in the arts is tantamount to death,"*[20] he didn't mean maybe. Nor did he mean that a motion picture or a fountain is superior to a statue or a still life. Intellectual immobility is the point to be made here, and this day it was to be written in blood.

More and more people began to notice that the SUV wasn't moving across the railroad tracks as automobiles usually do. They were beginning to notice the *stasis*.

The position of the SUV at a point crossing four parallel lines would not, by itself, be a matter of any concern—were it not for the ominous *stasis*—which made it a focus of immediate import. In the midst of the aforementioned stasis, the stalled SUV became a determinant object that would fuse two trains running fast in opposite directions; trains that would normally pass each other by in a blur barely noticed; trains but for the riveting crux of the looming stasis would never meet—but might now be forever fused in the horror of a backbreaking collision.

Men and women began shouting and yelling, and I think that Zilch and I were among them, but we were all immediately aware that there was nothing that any of us could do but watch—that is, to watch with increasing alarm as raw fear turned to panic and dread. I am certain that there were doctors and lawyers and carpenters and engineers and mechanics in attendance, not to mention the captains of industry, and

---

20   Marsh, *Rhetorical stasis theory.*

there were people of every nation and race and creed on the railway platform—after all, this was happening in Los Angeles. But shout as we might, as we would, as we did, we did nothing to mitigate the stasis.

It simply stood as an inalienable fact, which we moderns have become accustomed to dealing with. It simply stood as an existential reality, along with the triumphs of our language and our logic and our vastly improved selves. It simply stood on the tracks as the sounds of the engines bore down, as we stood with our own stasis showing.

Oh, this was an accident waiting to happen if ever misfortune were waiting. And we might try and skip over what comes next—to dismiss it as with the turn of a page and shine on with our lives safe and sound. But then we would be missing the idea of sublime purpose at hand, the primary element of culture that is purposely hidden in the language of the text.

By this, I do not mean the lofty science of linguistic ontogenetics, which takes an anthropological approach to understanding societal behavior in relation to its language's system of reproduction. For such eminent scientists tend to focus on the word as a symbol of society's unconscious cultural projection of itself through its language and would thereby propose that the answer to a society's survival is to be found in the word-structure of its language. This might be all well and good for the classroom, wherein we entertain the ephemeral fantasies of youth, but to boldly declare that *the symbol is an abstraction of mind over matter* and then offer such an interpretation to those of us quaking on the platform might be considered somewhat superfluous—certainly less powerful than a locomotive.

For those of us on the platform, unable to do anything but gasp— let alone to reflect on the value of literature and its symbolic language as it might apply in such cases as this—we immediately found ourselves in a modernistic predicament much like that of dear Alice in *Through the Looking Glass.*[21] Despite running her fastest, Alice observes that she hasn't moved one bit. The Red Queen, a metaphysical counselor of sorts, tells her, "*Now, here, you see, it takes all the running you can do, to keep in the same place. If you want to get somewhere else, you must run at least twice as fast as that!*" Indeed, one could parse these sentences in

---

21   Lewis Carroll's sequel to *Alice's Adventures in Wonderland.*

an effort to gain certain insights into the time (now), the place (here), the theme (vision) of the drama, etc, etc. Vision, of course, being preeminent in accounts of modernity and modernism. "*No, no! The adventures first,*" advised the mythopoetically-minded Gryphon, and here I must agree, for "*explanations take such a dreadful time.*"

To the amazement of all, as the concurrence of two commuter trains approaches, each one traveling in equally opposite directions, a door opens, and a man scrambles out, leaving the sport utility vehicle on the railroad tracks. A door opens, and a man scrambles out, leaving all our expectations of normalcy and decency and causality at risk. A door opens, and a man scrambles out, leaving culture itself straining like a damsel in distress. In the hyperreality of this particular town, a door opens, and a man scrambles out, so as not to miss the impending spectacle.

At this moment, our stasis was shattered into oblivion. Just try and imagine the horror of two double-deck commuter trains colliding one with the other, both carrying hundreds of passengers who are all yet unaware of the annihilating fate that was about to come. But don't stop there; it gets worse. During the slow agonizing motion of the actual collision, one of the trains overturns, and the other one catches fire. You must include the breaking of bones, the spinal cord injuries, head injuries, and lacerations to unspeakable parts of their bodies. Some passengers are killed instantly, others are burned severely, and still others are left languishing in the most terminal stages of dying. The screams of steel scraping upon steel would be deafening. The fulminating detonation of an explosion in such close proximity would be terrifying. And the protracted crashing and grinding, devastating all that was once considered solid and secure, would serve to convince the most hardened of individuals that fate and doom are synonymous.

In the midst of the commotion, the shrieks, and the crashing, I realized that Zilch was no longer standing there beside me. I whirled around to see where he had gone, only to find that the man had collapsed on the platform in a heap. Trying to protect Zilch from the stampeding footsteps of the crowd, I called out to the driver to get the limo. I knew that the ambulances, which would no doubt arrive in the aftermath, would have much urgent work cut out for them. I suspected a heart attack and felt for the pulse.

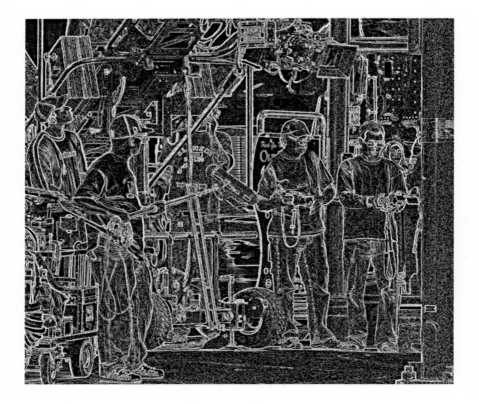

9. Twilight of the Egoists

The frantic limo ride to the hospital was like a classic chase scene in an action film, with the singular exception that we were being chased by the inescapable pall of death. Reeling and swerving from Glendale on San Fernando Boulevard to Silver Lake, we raced said pall, with the black velvet plumes of the train wreck spreading out behind us like a shroud over a coffin or a tomb, careening onto Hyperion Avenue and accelerating past the old Disney studios with the limo driver displaying considerable stunt driving skills, as well as frighteningly white knuckles, while I was coursing back and forth and occasionally sideways over the front seat while trying to apply real-time CPR to an unconscious Zilch, not knowing whether he needed it or not. It turned out that Zilch definitely needed it, but I didn't find that out until we actually arrived at the Hollywood Presbyterian Medical Center, formally known as the Queen of Angels.

Our arrival, of course, was just in time.

From there, it was a downward spiral of events, only some of which bear mentioning here, for modern medical care has, unfortunately, not developed quite as rapidly as one might have expected in the twenty-first century, certainly not to the same extent as other fields of industry or high technology or even public communication and cinematography, if truth be told. I knew that the best thing I could do for my client was to seek and find his precious Blue Dahlia, to inform her of the true seriousness of his circumstances, and to convince her to come to him, while the life and times of Zilch the man were still hanging by a thread.

I only had the address in the Pacific Palisades to go on, and I needed to get to my wheels. Heading up Vermont Avenue to Los Feliz in a hurry, I began to appreciate the axiom of predicate calculus which states that the number of city blocks one can run without stopping is inversely proportional to the number of cigarettes one used to smoke in a day. In no time at all, I found myself gasping and walking uphill in a full sweat. It would have been a perfectly beautiful day for a walk, were it not for the darker shade of realism rising and spreading like a cloak over the hills of Griffith Park, carrying with it the acrid smell of an industrial fire, along with the alienation, disorientation, danger, and oppression, not to mention darkness and gloom, that is more characteristic of an old film noir than a Hollywood script du jour. When I arrived back at my office, the same azure blue Ferrari California was parked there, waiting to be put to good use.

"*Cherchez la femme!*" I said to myself as I headed the coach toward the coast. "*Cherchez la femme!*" I repeated the mantra, spurring the Prancing Horse on to a low-flying gallop. The hillside mansions of old Los Feliz sped by as it would in a dream. The locations of studios, landmarks, and icons all blurred into oneness as I sped onto the pavements of Hollywood and Sunset and beyond, as doeth the distinctiveness of the stars.

"*Cherchez la femme!*" I drove on with abandon while death was starring at me in the rearview mirror. The thought that I might be driving beyond my own abilities and into a darker zone from which there would be *no way out* did not even occur to me, that is, until I realized that the mantra itself had altered its course: "*Cherchez la femme fatale!*"

Thankfully, I managed to arrive unharmed and without the entire LA police force driving behind me like a funereal procession in fast forward. The door to the house was locked up tight this time, and not being either a cat burglar or a bona fide private detective, I had only the natural instincts of a voyeur to rely on. Developed to an advanced degree over the years as an intrinsic part of my professional association with the private lives and theatrical performances of so many Hollywood celebrities, I felt quite comfortable peering into windows under even the most questionable and dubious of circumstances in order to gain a critic's unique perspective on the most private scenes imaginable.

There was no one in the interior shot; of that much I could be sure. The house was open and empty as a sound stage—I could see that clearly with my face pressed up against the perspicacious glass of the fourth wall. I heard the sounds of splashing that appeared to be coming from the pool area behind the house, but the redwood fences were too formidable to provide even a glimpse of the patio or the spectacular view of the coast from the front side of the building. Nor was my shouting met with anything but silence from what initially sounded like a pool party but was more likely to be the opportunistic bathing of some indigenous water birds.

It was desperation that made me do it, although it was among the very last things I wanted to do. I thumbed in Scarlett's number on my cell phone, setting the system to speaker in an effort to distance myself from the pain of our recent separation. I listened remotely to the sound of the phone ringing, thus removed.

"Hello, handsome," said the voice in the foreground, though the playful feminine salutation did nothing to lessen the sharpness of my phantom pain.

"Hello, angel," was all I could think to say. I was trying as hard as I could not to let on, not to let even one note be heard of the blind jealousy, the mixed emotions, and the aching feelings of disappointment that were welling up inside of me—again. "I need you to do me a favor, if it wouldn't be too much trouble."

"I liked you better when you played the hard guy for me … I mean, with me."

Oh, this was too much. Here she was, waltzing around town with a lame-brained assistant movie producer, dropping me like a stone, leaving behind all possibility of true romance for us, just to get a boost in her career—can you imagine? And now she was expecting me to behave like Sisyphus himself, expecting me to swallow my pride and roll the same stone up the steep hill again. Just how heroic can she expect me to be?

"You're the one who dropped the ball, angel. It was never up to me," I said. I wasn't feeling particularly heroic at the time.

"Well then, why are you calling me now?"

"Actually, I need to know where *Manifesta* is right now. It's really urgent, a matter of life and death, really. I can't explain it to you. I barely understand it myself. It's not for me is all I can tell you. Even if you don't take me seriously, please take this situation seriously. It's a matter of dramatic necessity!"

"Well, why didn't you say so, handsome? She's at the Hollywood Bowl as we speak, setting up for one of her magical creations."

"Thank you, Scarlett. You're a pal," I said, trying to distance myself again.

"While we're on the phone, there is one thing I'd like you to know," said Scarlett.

I swallowed hard and braced myself for the impact. "Yeah, what is it?"

"I really enjoyed our last kiss," she said. And then the connection went dead.

.   .   .

I used my season ticket, which comes with valet parking privileges, to gain access to the parking lot immediately adjacent to the Hollywood Bowl itself. There were enough people mulling around on various tasks, in preparation for the evening's performance, that simply *acting* like I knew what I was doing was sufficient to avoid suspicion. I entered the west gate of the outdoor amphitheater and strolled up to the terrace box seats. Manifesta was in discussions with an attentive bevy of engineer bees, while many others were swarming over an astounding array of computers and electronic equipment linked, apparently, and even by wires, to hundreds of projectors, reflectors flood lights, lasers, mirrors, stroboscopes, and who knows what else. Watching the woman work was, I dare say, a thing of beauty.

But I had an urgency of another matter on my mind. When she seemed satisfied for a moment that everything was progressing as she planned—as she directed—Manifesta sat down on the stage floor in the middle of the semicircular shell, or should I say, hive. It didn't take her long to notice me sitting alone in the box seats in front of her. It was mildly entertaining just to watch that strident manifestation of a woman rise up in her chic directorial attire and walk across the stage.

"Yes, Mister Philosopher to the Stars, what brings you here?" she said, approaching the marginalized cluster of folding chairs that comprise said terrace box seats.

"Haven't you heard?" I said. "There has been a terrible accident in Glendale. Two trains collided and jackknifed and burned. It's pandemonium to be sure. But that's not why I'm here. I need to talk to you about Kaltrina Dahl. I think that Zilch may be dying."

"Okay, you have five minutes," was all she said. As she started to walk away, Manifesta nodded her head slightly to one side in a succinct feminine gesture that said "follow me."

We ordered coffees at the walk-up counter of a small café aptly named Staccato. It was my second cup of coffee of a very alarming day, so I also ordered a butter croissant to help settle my stomach. We walked up the steps to the Rooftop Grill, which would formally open later for business, and we sat down at an unattended table under a big white umbrella that shaded the Southern California sun from our faces.

"May I ask what kind of performance you are preparing for the Bowl?" I inquired, more out of politeness than genuine interest.

"It's an introduction of my Virtual Avatar as a tribute to dead poets and composers. While the audience celebrates the cherished words and the music, it's my job to bring the artistic originators back to life."

"You mean you're going to project the images of composers in midair like the frightening alter ego of the original *Wizard of Oz?*"

Manifesta looked at me quizzically for an instant, as if she was trying to decide whether I was being sarcastic or simply coy. "Something like that," she said, almost smiling, "but I have added a few more dimensions."

"Not to mention that you have nearly done away with the man behind the curtains."

Judging from the change in her expression, Manifesta had just determined that I was anything but coy.

"Look, what I really came here to see you about is to get you to help me, to help Zilch."

"And how do you suggest that I could do that?" Manifesta asked in a tone that assured me she was no longer amused in the least.

"By convincing Kaltrina Dahl to see him again, before it's too late."

"I might have known," she said. "You men are always so predictable."

"Predictable or not, can you really deny the contribution that men like Zilch have made to the art of cinematography and to American culture. Can't you cut him some slack?"

"It's not my job to appreciate the past but to overcome the present."

The irony of her statement in relation to her current project notwithstanding, she was passionate and convincing wherever she shined her lights. I simply nodded.

Manifesta leaned forward as her discourse deepened. "Once upon a time, men wielded their pikes and swords, by choice, against real fears and real foes, or they chose to hide while others fought and died for causes that were worth fighting for. Then along comes a generation of *auteurs* who prefer to wave their undeveloped *anteocularium* at the silver screens in a futile gesture wherein a nostalgic pantomime of antiquated heroism is acted out and reenacted *ad nauseam*. The captive audience is entertained, maybe even impressed, but it is hardly captivated, it is rarely innervated, and it is almost never elevated. Men like Zilch gave us commercial entertainment as a substitute for real life, and neither men nor women are the better for it. Why should I cut him any slack?"

I attenuated my nodding so as to avoid the appearance of the automotive figurine and replied by paraphrasing Albert Einstein: "*To widen our circle of compassion to embrace all living creatures,* perhaps."

"If you must hurl your petty bromides at me, I prefer the soaring thoughts of Ralph Waldo Emerson, who was much more challenging and contentious. And I quote, '*But a compassion for that which is not and cannot be useful and lovely, is degrading and futile.*'"[22] Manifesta leaned back as if she hadn't a care.

"I'm not quite sure what you, or even Emerson, might mean by the term *useful.* Surely, you don't mean *practical,* as in pragmatism?" I gasped at the thought.

Manifesta reached into the front pocket of her skin-tight jeans and slowly withdrew a braided black thread, a braded black thread that was attached to a monocle, a monocle that soon found its way into the socket of a singular eye, a singular eye that was perceptibly enhanced by

---

22   Emerson's Address on *Emancipation.*

the magnification of the areola of its own iris. Once the conspicuous monocle was in place, she continued the conversation as before.

"Whether you realize it or not, there are still real wars going on—and by this, I don't mean petty skirmishes over oil fields. There are real wars raging all around us, moral wars of good and evil, cultural wars of antiquated ideologies, wars against needless suffering and illness, wars against the decadence and decay that festers within the very soul of man while your passive philosophies, your commercial enterprises, and your entertainment industries have collectively spawned a generation of feckless individuals who would run for the cure, walk for the cure, stand up for the cure, and now, owing to the feigned generosity of a local mattress salesman, they can even *sleep* for the cure. Lulled to passivity, modern man would rather climb the heights of meaninglessness and absurdity than actually participate in the most vital of wars. The rise and spread of such meaningless mass entertainment has fostered a passivity of culture that has lowered the bar of actual participation in life itself, lowered the bar to the point where it has effectively victimized much of humanity."

I filled my mouth with butter croissant as I strived to formulate a response.

"I understand, and indeed, I appreciate your passionate cultural agenda, but isn't it part of your responsibility as an influential filmmaker to show some appreciation for the fallen angels of the arts, particularly when you of all people know exactly what kind of power Zilch once wielded, how much he has lost in his fall from grace, and how little he now has left to defend himself with?" Unable to solicit any compassion for Zilch, I was trying, at least, for sympathy.

"It is my job to lead society forward with the banner and the flame of the intellect, with the resolve of an inspired artist, the courage of an indomitable warrior, and an eye for the mystery and the beauty of life that is unassailable by the corruption of the nations and the institutions of the world." Manifesta's widened eye flared with indignation. "The good old boys may wave their magic wands as wantonly as they like, but it is the womb of the woman where creation is made manifest. It is the womb of the woman where all life and art originates!" As she spoke with such fervor as to outshine the sun, I do believe she meant every word she said.

"With your focus so intently concentrated on the womb of the woman, might you be missing the essential sacrifices of the man?"

Manifesta paused for a moment as she sipped at her coffee, then she adjusted the monocle and continued. "As a man born and bred of psychology and philosophy, you should know, if you bother to look more critically behind the illusions, the mythologies, and the oral traditions you expound, there is a feminine *dream of beauty* that precedes and inspires the greatest of all such thoughts and deeds. Did it ever occur to you that the *real* story at the heart of Christianity itself is the love of a mother for her unborn child, a love that would bend nature and fate and destiny as well as the truth to such an extent that the whole world would be forced to suspend its disbelief?"

"No, but I assume you're going to try and convince me," I said, torn between premeditation and curiosity, staring into the newfound emptiness of my own paper cup.

Manifesta took a good hard squint at my predicament: my desire to attend to the immediate needs of my stricken client while denying my openness to the supreme dignity of her thoughts. She smiled at me like Mona Lisa herself. "Didn't it ever occur to you that Mother Mary created a better world for her child than the vulgar one she had inherited, better than the happenstance that had been *thrust* upon her?"

She paused for a pregnant moment and then continued. "For out of this tragic happenstance, Mary created a love story as a sublime act of will. She created the *dream of beauty* that led to the elevated value of the individual in society ... and it is this *dream of beauty* that led to the passion and the crucifixion and the renaissance and the endless reformations. Verily, I say to you, Mister Philosopher," she announced with her exaggerated eye flashing and flaring, "you might want to take a real good look at Michelangelo's *Pietà* before you even begin to tell me who gave what and to whom."

Philosophically speaking, I was trumped. Manifesta arose from the table like the *femme actuelle* she was, and she was proceeding to walk that way down the stairs when she hesitated. Graced by the stunning optical reflections of the midday sun, she turned back to me and offered a remarkably compassionate gesture.

"But I won't stand in your way if you try and convince Kaltrina Dahl yourself—that is, around midnight tonight."

. . .

In the neo-noir of a late summer's night, when the torrid breaths of the Santa Ana winds are high up in the trees and the shameless face of the moon is veiled by the ghostly galleons of darkness and intrigue and the looping road past Dead Man's Curve shines like a black ribbon threading its way through the lacework of a woman's negligee, the Prancing Horse came riding—riding—riding—with the Perspicuous Eye still driving, up to Kaltrina's door. This time, the door was cracked open, as it was the very first time.

Again, there appeared to be no one home. The rooms of the expansive modern masterpiece were nearly empty, as before. The fire was silently flickering in high definition on the flat screen in the background. The modern lounge chairs were empty, and the only reflections to be seen through the massive plate glass windows were either the emptiness within or the lights beyond, depending on the reflections and the angles of the strategic spotlighting.

Again, I heard the sounds of gentle splashing coming from the area of the pool. This time, I was determined to investigate, and although the interior of a modernistic home is not nearly as ergonomically and intuitively designed as a classic sports car, there was a general logic to the layout that guided me to the light switches that, ostensibly, would illuminate the entire scene—which I promptly proceeded to do.

There, appearing right before my eyes, glistening in the soft glow of the patio lights, was a more astonishing vision of loveliness than I have ever seen. Arising from the steps of the swimming pool with the grace of a goddess incarnate was a woman in what appeared to have once been a white leotard but was now moistened to the point of sheer invisibility, revealing every voluptuous curve of her exquisite form, every delectable nook, every evocative furrow and line that nature has drawn upon the body of woman was arising now from the most mysterious of waters whose limpid fingers seemed reluctant to release her from their grasp. The vision of loveliness moved in my direction to the very threshold of the patio doorway.

Her luminous beauty was as exotic as it was attractive, as graceful as a swan, as slender in parts where slender becomes sensuous, rising tastefully to a shapely plumpness which can only be described as luscious. Here before me, moving closer to me with every fluent step, was a beauty beyond compare: not to the majestic though severely chiseled countenance of the *Venus of Cyrene* nor to the stunning, threatening female pulchritude of Manifesta nor to the iconic pretentiousness of my aspiring Scarlett nor to any woman I have ever seen before this midnight's eve. And that's saying a lot in this particular town. There was no self-awareness about her exposure to my post-perspicuous eyes—it was if her composure were a form of radiance in and of itself. Her effect on my senses was clearly hypnotic as she approached so near to where I stood. Her dripping, shining, emanating, overwhelming beauty was, in a word, compelling.

"Kaltrina?" I said, as I ventured a guess.

"Yes, Joseph. I've been waiting a long time for you to find me."

"I feel like I've been waiting a lifetime," was all I could say.

"Do you have something you want to ask me, Joseph?"

If I had but one wish, in another world in which wishes were horses and dreamers could ride, it would be that this compelling vision before me, this luminous attraction that implores me, this rapturous feeling of desire to reach beyond myself to embrace and fulfill her every request, it would be that this enchanted moment would never end.

But such wishes are not for men like me, and I had a serious job to do. Try as I might to fall under the spell of her now and forever, I was charged with a motivation to find a purpose that was independent of my own personal desires. And although Zilch was not, perhaps, the most noble creature on the face of the earth, he was my client. He had sought me out from all the other theoretical possibilities, and he had considerable time and patience and trust invested in me. I simply could not let Zilch down.

"Kaltrina, I must implore you to reconsider your separation from Zero Vaynilovich. I really think he might die. Are you fully aware of his predicament?"

"Oh, yes, Joseph. It is likely to be so. Of his predicament, I am fully informed."

"Then you must go to see him at the Queen of Angels Hospital before it's too late," I implored her, though her graceful demeanor remained virtually unchanged, even after the extreme urgency of my entreaties was expounded.

"I have already made my rounds to the hospitals of Los Angeles, and this time my venue of choice was the Hospital of the Sick Children. The angels there are always so innocent, and there was a situation that needed my inspiration, as it were." Kaltrina's cool, calm demeanor was somewhat incongruent to my expectations of dramatic context, and her unclad candor in the face of disaster was dizzying to be sure.

"May I ask what kind of *situation* takes precedence over the life and death of Zilch?" At this point, I was feeling somewhat heroic in my struggle not to faint.

"In the most hopeless and tragic of situations, there is always one who refuses to surrender to circumstances. In this case, at the Hospital of the Sick Children, there were two. It's is not always the ones that are the most obvious, and it's hard enough even to find just the right one. It's really quite rare to find such a perfect pair."

The sublime thoughts she was exposing did nothing to obscure the more outstanding qualities of the brilliant Blue Dahlia that confronted me *au naturel*.

I was about to ask her, "Two of what?" when she continued on with her thoughts.

"It's even better when I manage to inspire mutual cooperativity in a given situation. It harkens to the fundamental dualism of nature." The soft and subtle patio lights did nothing to diminish the fullness of her assertion.

At this delicate point in the investigation, I had no idea what Kaltrina was talking about, other than the fundamental dualism of nature is a concept that anyone with vision of her embodiment could readily grasp. I summoned all my powers of concentration and professionalism and attempted to intercede on behalf of my client.

"Heaven knows your intents of *that pair* for the children, and I for one approve, but couldn't you find it again in your heart of hearts to offer one last embrace to the sorrowful man *in extremis*."

"I'm sorry, Joseph. That's not possible. Zero, you see, has become enamored—and unfortunately, not of me. He has become enamored of his style, his words, his works, his techniques, and his accomplishments, and I'm afraid that such situations are inevitably terminal." The vision of loveliness remained poised and dripping at the threshold.

"Is there nothing I can say as his counselor to make you change your mind?"

"Unfortunately, no. My sisters and I are nothing if not selective. But you might consider offering something of your own accord."

Ah, here was an opening that I might explore—on behalf of my client, of course. It appeared to me for the very first time that Kaltrina was as vain as any of the lesser gods, and therein lay my only chance to steer her back to said Zero.

"I'd like to meet any one of your sisters if they're anything at all like you," I bodily declared with all the professionalism I could muster under the circumstances.

"That's just flattery, Joseph Metropolis, and you might think that it's charming, even charming enough to advance your cause, but it is not. And it is not the least bit impressive to me, or to any one of my sisters. As I told you, we are terribly selective. You might even say we are selective to a fault." Bathed in the transparency of the patio spotlights, anointed by the mystery of the surrounding moonlight, such faults were not easily discerned.

The absurdity of the argument I found myself engaged in was as formidable as the illustrious beauty arrayed in all its perfection before my waking eyes. Kaltrina Dahl was more poised in her innate purity and more comfortable in her resplendent nakedness than I was with all my philosophies. I found myself increasingly attracted to her enchanting aphorisms, and for the sake of a newfound discretion, I silenced all my devious thoughts.

The silence might have lasted a minute or an eternity, it mattered not to me. But when she gazed so deeply into the depths of my eyes and merely smiled, I was flooded with endless seas.

"Do you have something you want to ask me, Joseph?" she inquired, like a repetition of a riddle.

"I think so, but I'm afraid," I heard myself saying. I sounded so young and foolish.

She simply smiled again and told me that "primal fear is the beginning of wisdom," at least I think she was speaking. By now I wasn't too sure. She was drawing me out with the obvious attractiveness of her voluptuous being while casting me back to a time of pure, unadulterated innocence. Standing before her, I was a child.

I remembered the music, the place, and the time of my youth. It was clear as the sweet kiss of spring. I was standing alone at a teenagers' dance, but I was much younger than that. The beautiful child who had invited me there was standing an eternity away. The lace of her party dress, the patent leather of her shoes, and the plastic crown on her head were as vivid now as they were then. The girl-child's older sister and all her sister's friends were dancing with confidence and ecstasy and abandon, as were the majority of the young men in attendance.

But for me, this was all before the heat of the rut, before amorous experience guided, before there was any sophistication to my sex, and I stood not like a young man, but a statue of a young boy frozen in a park with the leaves of perpetuity falling. The space between the beautiful girl-child and the reluctant boy was a chasm that was far too dangerous to cross. There was too much personal interest to be had in the toes of my own shoes, not to mention the seriousness of intent and concentration required to attend to the hanging shard of a thumb nail.

"Do you have something you want to ask me, Joseph?" came the riddle again to my mind.

"Yes, but I need your help," I heard my child's heart speaking. All I could see were those eyes that belonged to heaven. All I could feel was the comfort of that smile that carried me along with its warmth. All I could sense was that ever-blossoming beauty that compelled me to rise to its elevated perspective.

"And who do you think inspires the child to span the vast spaces of desire? Who do you think inspires the man to take those first bold steps into even greater unknowns?"

"Yes, I remember. They were awkward steps; they were tremulous steps," I heard myself speaking to Kaltrina out loud.

"Awkward, yes, tremulous, yes … but to me, they were always endearing. Don't you remember what it is you asked me? It was very nearly, but not exactly, like a prayer."

"Yes, I remember now. It was almost like that, but not exactly. It was more like a moment, in the loneliest of moments, in the most perilous of moments, in the most compelling of moments, when you dare to reach out and you care enough to discover that you are very nearly, but not entirely, alone in your most superlative of desires."

"Now that you remember, do you have something you want to ask me, Joseph?"

"Yes, Kaltrina, there certainly is. I would … I would … I would *love* …"

And then there was an exaltation of sorts, as if it were the beginning of time when an entire universe explodes into existence or a monk climbs a dark mountain at the brink of a sunrise or a full-grown philosopher, for the love of wisdom, reaches out with his arms to embrace the eternal beauty before him, with his heart upon his sleeve.

It was at that very moment that Manifesta, delayed, perhaps, by an extended number of appreciative encores at the Hollywood Bowl, happened to arrive back home.

•   •   •

It's a touchy situation under the best of circumstances. However, in this case, the coldness of the atmosphere, not to mention Manifesta's stare, was somewhat exacerbated by the realization that the entire front of my shirt and my pants were clearly soaking wet.

"You men are so damn predictable! I believe I even warned you about this!"

Given my somewhat soggy situation, and the inherent ponderousness of any conceivable explanation, I hesitated to say a word, although I must say that I was beginning to feel a curious enervation from the epic beauty at hand.

"Welcome home, Mani dear," said Kaltrina in the calmest of voices. "Did Ludwig van Beethoven manage to roll over during the performance as you planned?"

"I had the old boy doing backflips," was all Manifesta said.

It was a most unconventional triangle the three of us made, even in the most modern of settings. Manifesta was dressed in a formal conductor's tuxedo, which did nothing to hide the flaming femininity that issued from every crease. I myself had been reduced from the august regality of my scholarly profession to that of a child who had been caught with his hand in the proverbial cookie jar—only worse, for I wasn't a child. While Kaltrina Dahl simply stood there with the unruffled radiance of a prima ballerina, completely aloof to all the untoward emotions that were raging beneath the surface.

I began to wonder if any of us had the least bit of sympathy for the passing maestro of drama and cinematography who had taken us from the classic mythologies to the very cusp, if not the pinnacle, of our current modernity. I felt a definitive pang of regret, if not responsibility, to try and ease his constant suffering and his unbearable sadness by attempting, at the very least, to bring him the answer to the mystery that he had originally engaged me to uncover. At least someone was still thinking about Zilch.

"Kaltrina, may I see you for a moment in private?" asked Manifesta with remarkable civility, though I could sense a certain strain in her voice.

"Of course you can, dear Mani," said Kaltrina.

And they left me alone in the room.

Now a Perspicuous Eye, even one with very damp clothes, is nothing if not discrete. I wandered out to the pool area, clicking off the patio lights as I did so. There in the misty moonlight of the coast, with the Santa Anna winds high up in the trees, I began to examine the chaparral of the hillside habitat and the attenuated purviews of city lights somewhere off in the distance. Still, I could hear the sounds of an argument, heavily punctuated, that is, with occasional harsh tones. After a while, the silence returned—it was just me and the wind and the trees.

"You'll have to excuse me, Doctor Metropolis. Apparently, jealously comes with the territory."

It was Manifesta alone who had joined me by the poolside. Even in the veiled moonlight, I could tell that she had been crying by the lucent traces of tearstains on her hyper-feminine cheeks.

"I'm sorry if I caused you any—" I was beginning to apologize, but she cut me off.

"Oh, it's not entirely your fault," she said. "Muses are nothing if not promiscuous, and Kaltrina is no exception. It just annoys me no end when I think … when I realize … that my work is just beginning."

I decided that the best course of action in this ongoing investigation of mine would be to let the woman speak for herself, without any prompting from me.

"When I think of all the time and effort I put into this relationship—all the personal sacrifices she demanded of me—all the mindless adoration—all the attention to each and every detail of her instructions, however counterintuitive, however illogical, however quaint, however precious, it makes me furious." Leaning on a railing overlooking the cliff edge and the city, Manifesta stood defiant, her dark hair tousled by the gathering breezes of the sea, her tearstained cheeks faintly illuminated by the soft, yellow light of the moon. "After all, it was my brain, my mind, my heart on the anvil!" She stood fierce and tall. "It was my will that was done after all. How dare she turn her face to another. How dare she. How dare she turn that beatific face from me! From *me*!"

Suddenly, there was the thunderous sound of a door slamming finally in the background while a grief-stricken Manifesta reaches for and touches her empty tearstreaked eye socket, a door slamming finally with a singular, thunderous clap.

10. Luminous Stars Die Superbly

It is a law of physics that massive stars burn brighter than most for a relatively brief period of time, and then they tend to die dramatically in a spectacularly creative manner. It's strange to think that the golden earrings and necklaces worn on the red carpet each year were made possible by the flamboyant death of a previous superstar, but it's true. You see, the gold that is mined from the bowels of the earth and purified and melted and molded into objects of such adornment was not created here, nor was it created in the hypothetical "big bang" that spawned the universe at the beginning of time as we know it. The gold and the platinum we treasure, along with the uranium and plutonium we dread, and, indeed, all the other elements that are anatomically heavier than iron, were not created gradually or *chronologically* in time but were born in the *kairos* time of a significant moment, that is, at the very moment when a Great Star dies.

I was thinking of the parallels of these natural laws with various rhetorical schemata in which the term *kairos* represents a passing instant of time and space where something of great importance will be delivered. It is that *crucial time* when an opening appears that must be driven through with significant force if anything meaningful is to be achieved. As a philosophical practitioner with a client *in extremis* and an unfinished job to attend to, I knew that the appointed time of *kairosis* was fast approaching. Poised at the threshold of death's door, the gravity of Zilch's immediate circumstances had to be considered within the context of the luminosity of his life's work, which was once arrayed in glory upon the silver screen and is now available as reruns for all the world to see. It seemed to me that there was a parallel, or symmetry, if you would, between the natural laws of the universe and the unsolved mystery at hand.

If you would allow me to elaborate before too hastily turning the pages, I promise to proceed to the main point with restraint and brevity. You see, the creative alchemy of the universe dictates that a star's mass is proportional to its luminosity, and its luminosity is proportional to its performance. Whereas meager stars like our vainglorious sun follow an ordinary sequence of celestial events—burning hydrogen and helium largely and emitting the dull yellow glow we all find so comforting—that is, until these elemental gases run out and the whole thing collapses, leaving nothing but a gigantic carbon cinder glowing ever so dimly in a slow fade to black.

But the Massive Stars are different from yours and mine. They burn much brighter than does our little sun, but they cannot last nearly as long. They consume not only the noble gases, but the sooty carbon cinders, the sulfurous brimstones, the phosphorescent scintilla, and all the elemental amalgams of creative composition that can be conjured and wrought up to the point of situational irony, from which they can go no further. Not even a Great Star can thrive on dramatic irony for long—and that's when relentless gravity prevails over great luminosity. The ironic hulk of a massive burned-out star invariably collapses upon itself in a terrifically dramatic fashion, producing a Supernova. And it is in these Supernovae, in the crushing agonies of Great Stars dying, that all the heavier elements, including the shards of illustrious gold, are fused and derived as they are blasted to smithereens and stardust that spreads out and gathers like so many dust bunnies in the far corners of the universe; that is, until the dusty mélange eventually begins to ensemble with other smithereens and stardust in the eternally recurrent stage play of another cosmopolite studio.

All the so-called "heavy" and the "precious" and even the "transitional" metals were not produced instantaneously or gradually or even progressively, but in these decisive epochs of dramatic creativity that extend over vast eons of time. In other words—and more directly to the point at hand—Art, like the creation of substantial matter, like evolution of life on earth, is not incrementally, interminably progressive. No, indeed, it is punctuated; it is episodic; it is remarkably dramatic; it is propelled in fits and starts across a vast trajectory, like a flaming arrow, like a wild, unruly chariot racing at breakneck speed across the heavens with the brilliance of some distant inspiring, expiring sun ... leaving not but sublime traces of the great awakening in its wake.

If you would bear with these outlandish thoughts for an additional moment or two, I would attempt to explain how it is that the most gifted of theoretical physicists from dear old Einstein to poor dear Hawking admit that they are completely at a loss. Try as they might—and believe me, many have tried with *all* their might—to construe a grand and glorious formula that would indelibly place all the forces of nature onto a single page, or even a book of pages, they inevitably fail to do so. While space and time, the strong forces of atomic bonds, and even the vibrations of electromagnetism are well enough behaved, it is the very weakness of gravity itself that remains so treacherously problematic— and therein lies the rub. The grand unified theory of everything that continues to elude the most brilliant of theoretical physicists is a problem of gravity at its very core. Conceptually, Herman Hesse presaged this dilemma of our increasingly vacuous modernity with his playful yet ponderous magnum opus entitled *Das Glasperlenspiel*, literally, the glass bead game. More recently, and much to our relief, the logic and mathematics of modern science have managed to tether these troublesome illusive glass beads to a gossamer thread, with the invention of "strings" and "superstrings" that are supposed to hold everything imaginable together.

Alas, greater minds than mine have come and gone like waves upon the shores and still we have no answers to the very problem of causality that I have been contracted to address. We appear to have become bridled and bound-up unto ourselves like one of Kristophales' sadistically shrouded monuments while the elemental forces and creative impulses of the entire natural universe continue to elude our grasp. Thus the unsolved case of *The Lost Love of the Latest Tycoon* was weighing heavily on my mind. The more I thought about it, the more I became convinced that the plight of Zero Vaynilovich is nothing if not dramatic.

From what I could glean from the scribes in the utmost temples of modern science, including quantum mechanics and astrophysics, there are more *dimensions* in heaven and earth than have been dreamt of in all our philosophies. Really, truly, I kid you not. It is no longer a matter of vague speculation. The very best minds at this very moment in history are, for the first time, all in accord: we need to add more *dimensions* to the matter at hand and the space and the time and the quarks with their charm. In fact, it is formally proposed that the paltry number of dimensions of our existence must absolutely, positively, necessarily be increased to eleven, while there is not one shred of evidence to support such a hyperbolic contention.

Well, as long as we moderns—who have done away with the fomenting corpses of man's superstitions—have the academic entitlement to speculate upon such esoteric things as *unappreciated dimensions*, which would give us, shall I say, in the words of F. Scott Fitzgerald, *"The Whole Equation,"*[23] I feel comfortable enough with speculative thinking to venture a thought of my own. In point of fact— now that I have rubbed up against the lovely underlying impetus of the *true inspiration* in this case—I am brimming with such wholehearted inspirations as love and desire and aspiration. But if I had to venture but one *dimension* of my very own to add to the august annals of science and philosophy, not to mention investigative reporting and philosophical counseling, it would be the illusive dimension of **Drama** that is so often overlooked.

• • •

Despite the best of intentions and the best treatments that modern medicine had to offer, Zilch was clearly no better. Every day, he would wake with a glimmer of a promise of her return, only to have it gradually eroded as the days and weeks slowly passed one into another. I was beginning to wonder how much suffering a tragic hero could be expected to endure. I visited Zilch's hospital room every other day and watched with a sense of helplessness as his belief in his own freedom, his supreme pride, his sense of directorial commitment, his vigorous protests, were slowly fading away. There were times when I was amazed at the man's capacity for suffering. It was almost as if this sorrowful pathos was destined to be his greatest work of art.

I met with Manifesta on another occasion, sans Kaltrina Dahl. She was busy with the preparations and negotiations required for an

---

23   F. Scott Fitzgerald's unfinished novel *The Love of the Last Tycoon*.

upcoming collaboration with a major motion picture studio. When I asked her about her prior reluctance to use SAG actors in her redundant snuff films, in defiance of *Global Rule One*—hoping to hear anything at all about Scarlett—she explained to me that there was a problem with psychological and medical issues involving human resources and that this problem had been addressed more conveniently by joining rather than beating all the dead horses so to speak.

When I asked Manifesta directly, she said that Scarlett had become somewhat disillusioned with the diminishing returns of her acting career and that she hadn't given up entirely but was currently *pretending* to be a waitress at a club on the Sunset Strip.

Manifesta looked more frazzled and distracted than I remembered her as she explained to me the many challenges that the new media posed to directors and producers in Hollywood—what with changing venues and distribution channels, not to mention the emerging global markets; nothing would ever be the same. It was clear to me that her marvelous defiant edge was somewhat less marvelous these days. Her artistic eye was noticeably less keen without the glaring magnificence of the monocle. Her strident, provocative femininity was just a little less provocative, from my perspicuous point of view. It appeared to me that she might have mastered the *whole equation of pictures* in the meantime, but I for one liked her much better when she was the flaming and the flammable, the inspired and the inspiring, provocateur in love.

I wandered the streets alone at night, eschewing my borrowed wheels. I raised my collar to the dread of night and walked the walk, a miserable monad in the dark. In the gathering claustrophobia of my own mind, I was becoming too comfortable for my own liking with the same confusion of romance, pessimism, and alienation of the doom that haunted so many of my previous clients. In a world where everything is continually changing, where nothing is either stable or enduring, how could a mere juggler of scholarly mystique and ideologies possibly be of any service to himself, let alone to a dying society?

I was trying to figure out what I could say to a great man who was losing or had already lost everything he cared for and knew it all too well. What could I say without obvious criticism, without taking undue advantage, without one single solitary philosophical axe to grind?

I myself knew all too well that encouraging, mesmerizing, exalting influence that someone like Kaltrina Dahl could have upon a man—or a woman, for that matter. It was obvious to me that philosophy itself provides no protection from the muse as *femme fatale*. My feelings for all the creators she inspired were gradually melding into one of serious sympathy, along with a faint but discernable tincture of my own regret.

When it was determined that the end was near and there was nothing more to do, Zero Vaynilovich was moved back to his Beverly Hills palazzo with the accompaniment of a somber nursing staff. Not long after that, I received the urgent summons to his hospice scene that I never wanted to hear. Even the ride in the driver's seat of the latest supercar did nothing to diminish the increasing melancholy of my gloom.

He was lying in bed, propped up by pillows, surrounded by low-key lighting and the general silence of the nursing staff.

"With what more should I have come before my mislaid love?" asked Zilch when he first saw me.

I had no words of my own.

"How low should I have bowed down before my Blue Dahlia, the exalted eidolon who haunts my dreams?" he continued.

The eloquence of such destitution disarmed me, and I searched inside myself for truth. "It is my impression that all she wanted from you was that which you had yet to give, nothing more."

"Should I have come before her with burnt offerings, with a herd of sacrificial calves? Would she have been more pleased with the gift of a hundred handsome actors, or with ten thousand derricks pumping oil? Should I have offered up my admiring audiences for my prideful transgressions, the fruit of all my labors for the sins of my soul? Did she expect that more admiring audiences would be born posthumously?"

"I think you know exactly what she tried to show you, Mister Zilch," I said, moving close to the side of his bed. "I think you know what she considered the greatest good."

"Tell me anyway, in case I missed it."

"She wanted you to *think justly* and to appreciate the meaning of compassion and mercy, which she—above all—embodies with her endless love of man."

"Can you please be more clear, Metropolis? For my hearing as well as my sight seems to be fading from me."

I leaned closer in to the shadowy chiaroscuro of his face, and I spoke to him in a whisper. "I think she just wanted you to walk humbly by her side, to walk in the presence of the divine."

"Oh, is that all?"

"Yes, I think it is."

I stayed with him until the lights of his pale gray eyes went dim and the breath of his tortured soul finally let go of its inspiration. And then I left the palazzo.

11. Flight of the Great Muses

It had to end. I knew that from the beginning. But it may take me a while to recover from my own authentic sadness for the loss of Zero Vaynilovich. It's a good thing that Philosophical Counselors are not required to walk into the same funeral pyre as their dearly departed clientele, as was once the custom in many cultures around the world. While self-sacrifice may still be considered a virtue, even in modern times, self-immolation has slowly smoldered out of style.

I found myself wondering more often than before if it would not be possible for philosophy to benefit more than one individual patient—or rather, one individual client—at a time. I knew that scholarly books like my *Lost Angels Pantheon* had such a humanitarian purpose in mind, but the content of such literary endeavors was almost always limited to the collection of individual case studies hoisted upon discrete pedestals and bolstered by the lofty pillows of inductive logic to present a woefully generic though finely crafted can of worms. I found myself wondering if, indeed, philosophy could be raised once again to a more creative level, so to speak, by restoring the vital flame of wonder to the human mind and, by so doing, provide a guiding light for a society as great poetry once did, as great literature once did, as great works of art once did.

Though I found myself wondering such things more often than before—what with my latest client as dead as ancient history and my love life washed up on a deserted beach like a gutless abalone shell in the waning moonlight, with my mind increasingly clouded by a sense of meaninglessness and despair that comes upon me uninvited like the dampness of the marine layer and wraps itself around the world, leaving me, the gutless abalone shell, alone in the wet sandy muck while the tide is running out, leaving me with a hole in my chest big enough to put a lady's fist through—I had to dismiss these thoughts as the fading remnants of a brief but meaningful encounter with the likes of Kaltrina Dahl.

First you dream, and then you die. It is the title of the unfinished story of a life. My life, certainly. Perhaps even yours.

There were nights when I couldn't sleep at all. Nights when I would wander aimlessly along the hard concrete footpaths of the city in the solitude and the dark, passing strangers huddled in even darker recesses deep within their own locked doorways, strangers who would follow me briefly with their eyes blinking, hissing at me like angry cats, eyes squinting like stilettos at my every step or evading in trailing tones that disappear into the night like a police siren veering off in another direction, or worse, eyes that continue staring directly at me with a sustained expressionless silence that speaks to me of my failures with relentless disapproval, if not with complete contempt. Some nights have a thousand such eyes.

On a night like this, I would take to my reappropriated chariot, using speed to blur the faces that bore such eyes as these, speed that erases all unnecessary details in the periphery of the unfinished story of a life, a life like mine or perhaps even yours, a life that wages everything on the promise of a final act.

On a night like this, I had to get out of the city, and I had to get out fast, while it was still nice and dark. I took the 110 freeway— the oldest, most outdated freeway in all of California—and I took it with all possible speed. As the 110 winds its way from downtown Los Angeles past Chinatown and the Dodger Stadium to Pasadena, it becomes dangerous and narrow, and it makes you concentrate just to stay alive. I drove hard and fast, and it was just what I needed, for I managed to leave most of those thousand eyes far behind.

I pulled off at the Orange Grove exit at the outskirts of Pasadena to avoid unnecessary encounters. It was later than late, and there was no one else on the Millionaire's Mile, but speed was not the ticket in this part of town. On South Orange Grove Boulevard on the outskirts of Pasadena, the Victorian streetlamps are arrayed like big glowing eggs set on both sides of the road with such quaint proximity and precision as to be reminiscent of a carnival ride set in another place and time.

If you happen to cruise this boulevard at just the right speed and in just the right frame of mind, there is a surrealistic spectacle to be seen. However, on a night like this, in the dim and the darkness, there were stranger things about to happen and even stranger sights to behold.

I parked the well-heeled supercar on Grand Avenue just past that cliff-side monument to antiquity that was once the glamorous Vista Del Arroyo Hotel but was more recently refurbished into officious cubicles and relegated to the vagaries of justice in the form of the Court of Appeals. The grounds around the courtly old hotel were as deserted as a ghost town after the pay dirt has run out. I walked around the compound in the dark, feeling all kinds of sorry for myself and for others who had come to naught.

I followed the sidewalk around a bend and found myself entering onto the curious walkway of the Colorado Street Bridge, which curved out in front of me to the right. The stately old bridge was originally constructed at the turn of the last century but was abandoned for several years due to general neglect and an occasional earthquake, which had rendered it unsafe for human transportation. The elegant structure of the Beaux-Arts Bridge is evident even at night when the concrete arches disappear quickly into the stygian darkness of the Arroyo Seco down below. There is good reason that they call this the "Suicide Bridge," and it is believed to be haunted by hundreds of lost souls.

Once part of the original Route 66, the Colorado Street Bridge over the Arroyo Seco is like the ancient ruins of a classical stage, a reminder of times gone by. They built a brand new freeway to carry the traffic from Glendale through Eagle Rock and Pasadena to the east, so even though the folks of Pasadena raised the funds needed to restore the old bridge to its former glory, it remains a bridge less traveled by. On a night like this, when it is later than late and the concrete arches descend into darkness, the Beaux-Arts Bridge was virtually deserted, with the exception of a dispirited philosophical practitioner who found himself alone, lost in his own sorrow, without a single client.

The cast-iron lampposts each clutched an array of five glowing balls that shown like clusters of ill-illumined grapes, casting an aura of theatricality onto the surrounding darkness that was hardly diffused and more in keeping with the atmosphere of alienation, loneliness, and despair that I was feeling with the mournful application of each forsaken step. It was then that I heard a familiar voice and saw a radiant hallucination standing there before me with uncharacteristic warmth and expectation.

"So you're the one who is charged with managing one of the world's oldest, most deeply disturbing woes." The voice was familiar and lovely—neither inquisitive nor declarative, just familiar and lovely. "I have never met anyone who could even dream of doing such a wonderful thing."

There you have it. Just like that. One minute you're wallowing in the depths of your own despair, and the next you're confronted with a vision of loveliness colored with familiarity and expectations beyond compare. But I wasn't buying it. I wasn't buying any of it. Not at this point in the story, certainly not on a night like this.

"It's a bitter little world, but I wouldn't want to drown it with my philosophy," I found myself saying out loud. I wasn't feeling very *wonderful* at the time, and the imaginary dream girl before me was not nearly as convincing as the grim and dire reality of my current predicament.

"It is that very gentlemanly humility that makes you so useful, Mister Metropolitan Philosopher," said the soft, cool, familiar voice. "It is the very thing that qualifies you for this exalted road that you are on."

Speaking of roads, I noticed that I had wandered off the cement sidewalk and was standing quite precariously in the very center of the asphalt roadway. I whirled around to be sure that there were no headlights coming around the curves from either direction. I checked again—in cases of such vivid hallucinations, it's always better to be safe than sorry. There were no headlights moving on the bridge, only the globular clusters of lifeless streetlamps along the walkways and the vague reflections of bleak security lights around the empty Rose Bowl far off to the north and the intermittent drone of motorcars speeding along the modern freeway in the distance.

It was then that I heard the voice again and recognized it as that of Kaltrina Dahl.

"On the stage of life that remains before you, Joseph, shouldn't you consider the possibilities, the classic and dramatic possibilities, of one last dance?"

It was as if Kaltrina Dahl was already dancing right in front of me, elegantly, alluringly dancing, looking up at me with seductive feminine anticipation, and then not looking at me at all, in a most modern fashion of dancing. Moving erotically to and fro with irresistible provocations of inveiglement that commanded my immediate participation— yet alternating with moments of withdrawal and detachment that only served to make each successive rejoinder all the more enticing. Although I was not sure what was real or imagined at this point, I was sure that the ethereal beauty dancing before me was real enough for me to go with it.

Here was Kaltrina Dahl, dancing with me, a lowly philosopher, on a night like this, on a bridge less traveled by, flickering and fluttering in synchrony with my every movement while I was being enchanted to a state of mind that exists beyond all fascination. And that's when I began to hear the music that I recalled from another time so long ago. And that's when Kaltrina moved away far out of my reach and was replaced, almost instantaneously, by another young dream woman who I assumed to be one of her beatific sisters, a woman whose rhythmic concupiscent movements were even more irresistible, if such a thing is possible, drawing me even deeper into the fevered frenzy of the golden oldies that were spinning in my mind and the suggestive provocations of the most intimate forms of dancing.

There were more of Kaltrina's sisters than I can even recount, each one more becoming than the last, each one drawing me away from the edge of my own despair into the warmth of their amorous, rapturous, intoxicating, though all too transitory, embraces. In no time at all, I found myself surrounded by a fluttering bevy of beauties: tantalizing beauty, blossoming beauty, charismatic beauty, prepossessing beauty, overwhelming beauty, and the like. I was dancing with and in between and in among them all.

Now, I've heard the stories about the blessedness of suffering and the legends of heroes who were attended by angels, but this is ridiculous. I'm no hero, and I never really intended to be one—just another slob with a certain job to do; and my job just happens to be helping other people out of their misery. What could possibly be heroic about that?

However, on a night like this, when it's later than late and things have gotten considerably weirder than usual and you find yourself dancing with such irresistible beauty to music that couldn't be coming from anywhere else but your own imagination, I decided not to think about it any more. For one thing, I was beginning to feel kind of happy that I was even invited to this particular dance.

There I was, dancing on the center of the neoclassical bridge with a flock of the most beautiful creatures in the world, one by one, of course, when I began to notice that the beautiful young women were beginning to divest themselves of their earthly raiment, as it were, revealing a more sublime beauty that can only be described as *unearthly*. With each beauteous divestment, the feminine figures became more exquisite but perceptibly fainter and lighter and more luminous than the moment before. I searched the glowing whiteness for the dazzling face of Kaltrina Dahl, and finding her gossamery countenance, I followed it to the very edge of the Suicide Bridge.

"Kaltrina! Don't go!" I heard myself saying with a newfound *desperation* in my voice.

She turned and stilled me with an elegant gesture, which in her shining nakedness is hard for me to describe. "My sisters and I are rapidly disappearing from this modern world, as you can see, at the very edge of night. You know that we are well beyond the pale of an endangered species. We are very nearly, but not exactly, extinct."

"Very nearly, but not exactly—I remember clearly now. What can I do to convince you to stay a little longer? Please tell me, what can I do?"

Her radiant smile told me the answer, although it was not at all the classical answer that one might have previously conceived. A man might sacrifice himself out of grief or rail against nature itself as an evil villain, or worse, as a dirty trick, but here in the sublime resplendence of the fleeting beauty before me, I was acutely aware of the realm of the divine.

"You mean it would be best for me to love you from afar, as I love wisdom and beauty and truth?" I asked. But for me, it was no longer a question. It was fast becoming a necessity before my post-perspicuous eyes.

First you dream, and then you die. It is the title of the unfinished story of a life. My life, certainly. Perhaps even yours. I knew that I had entered this deserted bridge alone in the darkness of my own neo-noir and that, this remarkable ethereal beauty notwithstanding, I would end up alone again. However, if there was anything at all that I could do about it, I was going to make sure that I would never be quite the same.

Kaltrina was standing on the concrete bulwarks—preparing to climb up the rails and spikes that had been added to the original architecture during the renovations for the purposes of suicide prevention—when I could bear the thought no longer. I knew that I was reaching beyond all reason to hold on to the glory of the inspiration of an unfolding beauty that surges beneath the fabric and our language of our logic and our selves. I lunged over the traffic guardrail that separated me from the resplendent, voluptuous nakedness of the most luminous Blue Dahlia, and I pulled her down into my arms.

Kaltrina Dahl did not resist in the least. In point of fact, she embraced me with such purely passionate force, such moving, pleasing, sensuous insinuations that I hesitate to put my pen to paper, leaving instead the unchaste stir of voluptuous beauty in the innocent mind of the beholder.

"Kaltrina! Please! I'm not ready to live without your blessed inspiration. I know for certain that I can't do it alone!" I found myself pleading for the first time in my life.

"Dear, dear Joseph Metropolis, my dear woebegone Philosopher to the Stars, isn't it time for you to realize that it's enough for me that you try?"

I was flooded with every emotion a man can experience when he is in the arms of just the right woman, with just the right emotions, with just the right movements and just the right pressures for just the right amount of time as to bring forth such surges in creativity that might give rise to a thousand new Renaissances. Another moment and I was virtually dripping with the bittersweet alluvium of creativity. I held Kaltrina at arm's length to witness her own satisfaction when I was met with a pleasing smile that was not Kaltrina's at all but was the engaging smile of my aspiring Scarlett, which had moved me so on other notable occasions.

Before I could offer a verbal protest, which was hardly called for, considering the waves of sensuous satisfaction I was continuing to experience in fairly massive swells, Kaltrina herself, albeit with Scarlett's smile, whispered something decisive in my ear.

"You might consider taking Scarlett to the ballet sometime, Joseph. Even the darkest of swans can have its romantic compensations."

And then I knew it was time for me to let her go. It was more like an intuition than a signal—all the same, it was time to let her go. Suddenly, Kaltrina was no longer heavy and heaving in my arms, and though it is terribly hard for a man to let go of such a wondrous and enchanting dream of beauty, there can be no finer choice. I felt the unbearable lightness of her being as she delicately kissed my lips and folded something gently into my hand, and then she simply vanished into the luminous flux.

I didn't have to look to know what gift Kaltrina Dahl had placed into my hand. Some mysteries need not be solved with such *exactness*. Like all great gifts, one can assume that it is fragile and precious and fleeting, like life itself. My life, certainly. Perhaps even yours.

The night was just beginning to surrender its dominion to the twilight of the dawn when I crossed back over the graceful arches of the Colorado Street Bridge. I found myself thinking about Scarlett. I was thinking a lot about the unpleasantness of her history. But mostly, I was thinking about that smile—that smile she smiled just for me. Who knows? Maybe I'll give her a call.

Finis

12. Kommos (Epilogue of the Chorus)

Metropolis, Metropolis, Metropolis! El Metropolis de Los Angeles! Your once-guiding lights appear to have lost their candescence. The golden age of film has passed on into memories as the star machines that once launched a thousand heroes and heroines on voyages of the imagination have ground down to a merely degenerate preoccupation. Nowadays, there are only moth-eaten ghosts in the machine and petty politics and consumer demographics and reels of disillusionment. Thy modernization has spawned a generation of mediocre merchant-men too busy parsing the residuals in an industry of diminishing returns to contemplate the loss of their own inspiration.

What star have we postmoderns together fallen from to meet here at this impasse? Have we not sold our birthright of awe and wonder, laced with unbounded inventiveness and creativity, for the glimmering positivity of some laboriously constrained dialectic, along with the unequivocal certainty of our own superiority? When everyone in every hamlet becomes a countercaster, who among us remains to dig for nature's diamonds; who remains to mine the regenerate gold? Has not the grim reaper of our newly forged mentalities slain all possible forms of enthusiasm, leaving naught behind but scavengers who create nothing but more nothingness?

Our disdain for the old gods of creativity, if not the creators themselves, has come home to roost in every Metropolis. The divine inspiration of the graces and the muses that once brought radiance and joy and rejoicing to the various arts and sciences were among the first casualties of our abject postmodernism. No longer does Athena come to the architect Epeius in a dream to create the objet d'art that would turn the battle, and thus the war, and thus the course of history. The degradation of the aspiring, freedom-loving woman in our modern societies is but a symptom in relation to a far more insidious dis-ease.

And who but the lowly philosopher would dare to step dramatically upon such a worldly stage as this? And what would be his intent? He has but one intrinsic virtue to call his own: that is, his undying love of Sophia herself, as she is, as she ever was. And this is the dimension that is hereby added to "*the whole equation*" in the litany of postmodern man. For it is here in following carefully the steps of the intrepid philosopher—in his serious contemplation and ultimate re-vision of the eternal Dance of the Swans—that we find the unfortunate fissure of the *beautiful-ideal* from the *terribly-real* forever mended. His purposeful steps into Hollywood neo-noir are to redress that unhealed fracture of classicism and modernism, that gaping wound that separates our creative leaps of imagination from the dirgelike drudgery of our systematic progression with a strident promenade of enlivened aestheticism that is dramatically, psychologically, sociologically, and even philosophically profound.

It is not as unimportant as one might think, considering the wars we have at hand, for it is not only art and theater and drama at stake, but the most vulnerable parts of our societies that continue to languish on the chain of failed expectations. It is almost as if humanity itself hangs from the frayed remnants of this slender, gossamer thread.

Exit Chorus